NOTHING BUT A SONG

Keri De Deo

Crystal Publishing LLC
Fort Collins, Colorado

NOTHING BUT A SONG

Nothing but a Song

2018 ©COPYRIGHT Keri De Deo
2018 ©COVER COPYRIGHT Crystal Publishing LLC
Edited by Claire Shepherd
Cover design by LotusDesign.biz

Published by Crystal Publishing LLC
Fort Collins, Colorado

ISBN 978-1-942624-28-8
Library of Congress Control Number: 2017942671

For all people in the world who have a dream and to those who believed in mine

Rebecca Kendall waited for her boyfriend, Tommy Fletcher. She pushed her dark blonde hair behind her ears as she looked up and down the quiet suburban street. *Where is he?* she thought.

She considered messaging him but didn't want him texting while driving, so she kept her phone tucked in her jacket pocket.

Rebecca loved the fact that Tommy stood a good six inches taller than she. His muscular body would encircle her, and she felt safe in his arms. His perpetual smile always made her smile back. He was perfect. He was just never on time. Rebecca's mother didn't approve of him because he was 24, and Rebecca was only 19. They still went on dates, but Rebecca preferred to wait for him outside . . . less drama that way. She got off the steps and wandered around the damp grass soaking the bottom of her torn jeans and sandals. She laughed to herself as she remembered the little argument with her mother about wearing torn jeans on a date.

"You're not going to wear those silly things, are you?" her mother had asked.

"Sure. We're just going to a movie," Rebecca answered. That's the only thing they ever did. Tommy was working on his degree in film production, so he was obsessed with seeing just about every movie ever made. Tonight, they were going to see a sci-fi thriller about life on Mars. Rebecca wasn't that excited to see it, but she wanted to spend time with Tommy. Plus, they were taking the long way around to see the sunset from the top of Oak Creek Canyon.

"Well, you would think a gal your age would have enough sense to wear something decent."

"Oh, Mother . . . " she said as she rolled her eyes. Their arguments usually ended that way.

Her mother had shaken her head before walking back into the house.

It began to sprinkle again when Tommy drove up in his silver Hummer, and Rebecca ran to the curb to meet him.

"I thought you'd never get here," Rebecca said as she climbed into the giant SUV and closed the door. They kissed briefly before Tommy provided an explanation.

"Sorry 'bout that," he said.

"Why were you late?"

"My dad didn't want me driving tonight. There's a severe storm warning out. I reminded him I'm 24 and can do what I want. It was the same ol' argument . . . ya

know . . . 'not under my roof . . . blah, blah, blah . . . "'
He shrugged and pulled away from the curb. "I need to
find my own place! But here I am! Nothin' can happen
in this tank!" He pounded the dash to emphasize his
point.

"Great. I'm glad you convinced him. I was just
about to go back inside."

"A few drops won't hurt, but ya think it'd be all
rained out by now. Look at the size of those rain drops."

"Maybe we should just go to your house."

"Nah, I want to see this movie. Besides, my dad's
still pissed, I'm sure. I don't wanna deal with it."
Tommy turned on the radio and found a good station
as he merged onto Highway 89A.

The highway wound through the pine forest, and
the sun attempted to peek through the black and purple sky. The song on the radio played and beat in time
with the windshield wipers and the pelting rain.

As Rebecca rested her head on Tommy's shoulder,
a car veered into their lane.

"Tommy, watch out!" Rebecca screamed, and
Tommy jerked the steering wheel away from the on-
coming headlights. The tires lost traction. The car
spun out of control and off the edge. The guardrails,
meant to keep cars on the road, were no match for the
huge, silver Hummer as it crashed through the rail and
into the trees.

The passing car continued on its way, oblivious to
the carnage left behind.

Several minutes later, the blackness behind Rebecca's eyes receded, and she felt a jolt as the car
rocked on a branch. The SUV hung precariously over a

ravine—a large oak branch kept the car pinned above the canyon floor. She felt something cold and sticky coming from her ears and forehead. Touching it, her fingers came back bloody red. Her ears rang and her body ached as the seat belt dug into her chest keeping her from careening through the windshield.

To her left, Tommy slumped over the steering wheel—his eyes open and bleeding. Rebecca gasped and reached out to him, but pain shot up her arm, and she quickly withdrew.

The car lurched again, and Rebecca felt the sickening sense of falling as her vision blurred and then turned black. Luckily, she missed seeing the car as it plunged through the trees and landed on a rocky ledge. It left a tangled mass of dirt, flesh, and blood.

CHAPTER 2

The hospital was quiet. Time stood still as Jacob and Mary Kendall waited for news about Tommy and Rebecca. Jacob hardly fit in the plastic chairs. He crossed his long legs, uncrossed them, leaned forward, and rubbed his wispy white hair. Every now and then he would take his wife's small hand and squeeze it. She looked up at him with her soft brown eyes and crooked smile. Although her face didn't show it and her brown curly hair looked perfect, he knew Mary was worried.

Mr. Kendall stood up when Tommy's mother, Sue Fletcher, rushed through the sliding glass doors.

"Jacob, have you heard anything?" she asked him.

"No, we haven't," he answered and offered her a seat.

"Carl is parking the car," Mrs. Fletcher said as she took the seat next to Mary. They clutched hands and touched cheeks briefly.

The hospital doors slid open, and Mr. Fletcher squeezed through the opening before the doors allowed enough room for his large frame.

Mrs. Fletcher ran to Carl; he embraced his wife. "Any news?" he asked. Sue shook her head. Carl grasped Jacob's offered hand and nodded to Mary.

The doctor came in, and everyone stood. Carl thrust his large hand at the doctor and barked, "How's my boy, Doc?" The doctor frowned and asked if they could speak in private.

"Anything you say can be said in front of the Kendalls. They have a right to know, too." Sue said as she clutched her husband's hand.

"It's okay," Mary said. She patted Sue's arm and walked away with Jacob. They watched the trio vanish behind a wooden door.

On the other side of the door, Dr. Schmidt spoke softly. "Mrs. Fletcher, Mr. Fletcher, I'm sorry. I have bad news. Your son suffered extensive brain damage from the accident. He was unresponsive. I'm sorry. We could not revive him. There was nothing we could do."

"What?!" Sue cried. Carl put his arm around her.

"My boy is dead?" Carl asked, hugging his wife.

The doctor nodded and patted Carl's shoulder. "I'm so sorry," he said. "A social worker will be here soon to help you." He left the room and quietly closed the door.

Jacob and Mary approached Dr. Schmidt. "How . . . how's Rebecca?" Mrs. Kendall asked as she placed her hand on the doctor's arm.

He looked at her hand on his arm and motioned her to move away from the door.

"She's unconscious right now. She just got out of surgery. She had a brain hemmorhage, and we had to relieve the pressure. It will be a while before you can see her."

"But she's alive?" Mary asked, leaning into Jacob, who stood behind her.

The doctor nodded. "She's lucky. The driver's side took most of the impact. She has a severe head injury, but we won't know the extent of the damage until she's awake and we can run some tests. The nurse will come get you when you can see her. It might be a long wait. She's in recovery right now." The couple nodded and turned back to the waiting room.

A social worker in a blue and brown paisley skirt entered the room where the Fletchers were waiting. Mary caught a glimpse of Sue sobbing as Carl hugged her close to him. *Tommy must be dead*, Mary thought as she recalled the doctor's words: "The driver's side took most of the impact." She felt bad for the Fletchers but relieved about Rebecca.

Sue and Mary had known each other in high school, but they had not been close friends because Susan had graduated two years before Mary. They had had a crush on the same boy, but Sue graciously stayed out of the way. Still, their amicable association continued—one reason Mary allowed Rebecca to continue dating Tommy despite their age difference.

Mr. and Mrs. Kendall looked at each other. They squeezed each other and settled into the waiting room chairs for a long night.

♫♫♫

Hours later, a nurse in blue scrubs and squeaky white shoes approached the Kendalls. They could see Rebecca now.

As they followed the nurse to the room, she warned them, "She's still unconscious, but we think she'll be okay. The doctor had to drill some holes in her skull to relieve the swelling in her brain, so she'll have bandages on her head and drainage tubes attached. It looks bad, and it is, but her heart is strong."

The hospital resembled a small city with multiple floors and multiple buildings. In an attempt to make it look less like a hospital, the walls were painted peach and displayed calming pictures in random patterns. The doctors wore colored lab coats and dressed in business casual clothing—an attempt to make people feel at ease. Still, it was a hospital, and beeps resounded down the halls, hospital shoes squeaked on the heavily polished floor, and it smelled of disinfectant.

Jacob and Mary reached Rebecca's room; they pushed open the wide tan door.

Rebecca was asleep in her bed with the bed rails up. Her head was wrapped in bandages, and tubes fell around her, some with various colors of liquid inside. Her lips were moving, but her eyes were closed. Mrs. Kendall pulled a chair from the corner, sat down, and took Rebecca's hand. Mr. Kendall stayed standing at the foot of the bed.

Rebecca mumbled and moved her head back and forth. Her eyelids bounced as if she'd open them any minute, but she didn't. It would take time for her to wake up.

CHAPTER 3

A muffled ringing and a ripping pain brought Rebecca back to consciousness. The room was dark and silent. Her head pounded and felt like it was under water. Her surroundings looked unfamiliar and everything felt strange. Images flashed through her mind: driving, being pinned, seeing blood on her fingers, and seeing Tommy's eyes . . . She smelled burning rubber and smoke, and the feeling of imminent danger gripped her heart. She screamed.

The lights snapped on, and Rebecca saw a woman with red, curly hair wearing yellow scrubs enter the room. The nurse looked concerned. Rebecca's ears rang and pounded. She felt herself screaming off and on. The nurse didn't seem to react except to open and close her lips in strange formations. The piercing ringing in her ears continued, drowning out her thoughts and the nurse's voice.

She continued to scream . . .

"Tommy! Not Tommy! WHY?"

Her parents entered as the nurse pushed a syringe into Rebecca's IV. "What's going on?" they hollered above Rebecca's staccato screams.

"She's awake, but we need to sedate her. She'll rip out her stitches and the drainage tubes."

The syringe emptied, and the screaming stopped as Rebecca's eyes closed once again.

"But . . . " Mary stuttered . . . "she just woke up."

The nurse nodded and smiled. "It's a good sign. She just needs to rest. We'll try to wake her up slowly tomorrow. It's better if it's controlled. She needs to stay calm." The nurse put her hand on Mary's forearm. "Don't worry. It will be ok." Then she stripped her hands of the blue latex gloves after disposing the syringe in an orange bin.

"But who told her about Tommy?"

The nurse halted her exit and turned to Mary. "What do you mean?"

"Rebecca was screaming 'Not Tommy?' Did you tell her about Tommy?"

The nurse wrinkled her brow and shook her head. "No . . . " She looked at Rebecca and back at Jacob and Mary. "No. No one told her."

"Then . . . " Mary looked again at Rebecca. Totally confused, she stood there frozen in time and unable to utter another word.

♪♪♪

It was morning when the doctor arrived and slowly pushed liquid through Rebecca's IV as everyone surrounded her. Rebecca's eyes fluttered open a few minutes after the syringe emptied.

"Rebecca," Dr. Schmidt said in a kind, sing-song voice. "You're in the hospital."

She blinked and looked at the doctor as her eyes squinted in confusion.

One-by-one she looked at the faces surrounding her bed. "Wh . . . " she said and looked at her mom.

Mary smiled and nodded her head. "It's okay, honey. You've been in an accident, but you're okay."

Rebecca closed her eyes and shook her head while tears streamed down her face. "What's that noise?" She smothered her ears with her hands.

The doctor looked at the nurse and frowned. He pulled a light from his lab coat pocket and shined it in Rebecca's eyes.

Rebecca shied away but put her hands down and let him examine her.

"Excuse me," he said to Jacob and Mary, and the couple stepped away from the bed.

She kept her eyes on her mother. "What's going on?" she asked.

"You've been in an accident," the doctor repeated as he examined her ears.

"What did you say?" Rebecca said, looking puzzled.

"Rebecca, don't play games!" Mr. Kendall ordered.

Rebecca twisted her head, bewildered. She opened her mouth to speak and then closed it again. *What's the use?* she thought. She lay back and closed her eyes. Tears rolled down her face, and she begged the ringing in her ears to stop. If it didn't stop, she thought she'd die. *But I won't,* she thought, *not if Tommy's okay.*

"What's going on?" Jacob asked Dr. Schmidt as they left Rebecca's room.

The doctor looked back at Rebecca and closed the door. "It looks like there was some damage to her ears. It's really hard to tell the extent of the damage without more tests. But for now, your daughter can't hear. It could be temporary; it could be permanent. Let's stay positive and see what time will bring."

Jacob sighed and rubbed his hand over his face. He shook his head and then joined Mary at Rebecca's bedside. Rebecca kept her eyes closed.

♪♪♪

The next day, Rebecca sat in a hard, white chair in front of a white screen. Written instructions told her to hold her hand up when she heard a sound from the headphones she was wearing. A technician recorded her responses. It was difficult for her to hear anything with the incessant ringing in her ears, but she raised her hand when she thought she'd heard something besides the constant hum in her head. She had tried shaking her head and popping her ears as if she were in an airplane, but nothing helped. She hoped the doctor would have some news, but he looked as perplexed as she felt. As the day went on, her hope diminished.

Rebecca was sitting on the hospital bed when the doctor came to visit her and let her know the results of the test. Her parents sat close by.

The doctor came in with a pad of paper and a pencil, ready for lots of questions. "Hello, how are you feeling?" he wrote.

"Besides being deaf, I'm okay. Where's Tommy?" she asked on the pad of paper, not yet concerned about her own health.

"It's not a question of 'where,' it's 'how' you want to know," the doctor wrote.

"Right. How is he?"

"I want to tell you about the tests, first, Rebecca," the doctor wrote.

Rebecca looked at her parents. "Where's Tommy?" she wrote. Her parents both looked at each other and then looked to the doctor.

The doctor handed her the pad of paper with more of his writing.

"There's no easy way to tell you except straight out. Tommy's gone. He didn't survive the crash. Do you want to talk about it?"

Her parents were at her side, apparently aware of what the doctor had written.

"No, I don't. I'm kind of tired."

"I understand," the doctor wrote.

"Do you want to hear about the tests?" Rebecca shook her head and curled up on the bed with her back to the trio.

Her mother thrust the pad in Rebecca's face. "Rebecca, it's not your fault. Please don't pull away. We can help you."

She closed her eyes and shut out the world. It didn't seem a surprise that Tommy was dead. Somehow she knew . . . a dark memory haunted her at the edge of her sight, but she stopped it from floating into view. Instead, she rocked to the tone in her ears and cried. *I give up,* she thought. *He's dead. How could this happen?* Her thoughts tumbled as she fell deeper and deeper into sorrow. Her heartbeat slowed. She no longer had the nerve to live. *Why?* she kept asking herself. *Why Tommy?*

Jacob and Mary looked at Dr. Schmidt for answers.

"What can we do?" Mary asked.

The doctor shook his head. "She'll need some counseling. She has severe tinnitus and ruptured ear drums. The ear drums should heal in a few weeks, and we hope the tinnitus will go away, but it's really hard to tell."

"So, she's deaf," Jacob said, trying to come to terms with the new test results.

The doctor crossed his arms. "Well, yes and no. She reports having severe ringing in her ear, and she can hear some noises at a low frequency, but I'm not sure she really hears them or if she's just sensing vibrations. She'll need a specialist. I'll refer you to Dr. Talbot. He's an otologist, and he can give you some answers. Meanwhile, she needs to stay here until the swelling in her brain heals."

"What can we do in the meantime?" Mary asked.

"I'll get a social worker down here. He can recommend someone to help her learn sign language and cope with her new life."

"Is this permanent?" Mary gasped.

"We just don't know," Dr. Schmidt said. "I've never seen anything like this. With the damage to her ears and to her brain, it's hard to say if this is permanent or temporary. We'll just have to wait and see."

With that, the doctor left the room and left Jacob and Mary staring at Rebecca's back. Her rib cage rose and fell, and that at least gave them some comfort.

CHAPTER 4

"Rebecca's been home for weeks, and she's done nothing but mope around," Mr. Kendall told his wife at the breakfast table. "Mary, I know she's strong, but I don't know if she can handle this."

"I think she can, but what can we do? The social worker said that it would take time to adapt."

"She won't even talk to the doctors. The psychiatrist says she just sits in his office and stares at him or out the window. It's like she's completely shut down. I feel so hopeless. We have to do something."

"Jacob, don't worry. We have the best doctors. Dr. Talbot said all we can do is wait and see. Maybe we can get a tutor. We can get her to at least use sign language."

"We can work it out, but I'm worried." Jacob shook his head and pushed his cereal away from him. "Look, we're facing more budget cuts at the college this year, and they're cutting our health benefits. I just don't know what more we can afford."

Mary sighed, sipped her coffee, and then set it down, turning the handle back and forth as she breathed.

"I could call Dr. Talbot today and see what he suggests. I could also see if I can get more work at the antique store."

"Okay. We'll start with Dr. Talbot and see what he recommends."

♫♫♫

Mrs. Kendall was clearing the table when Rebecca came down the back, narrow stairs that entered the kitchen.

Rebecca had been in her room debating whether to come downstairs or not. It had been weeks since she got home from the hospital, and she was tired of being poked and prodded like some science experiment without getting any answers. She wanted to be left alone, but at the same time, she felt antsy and wanted to be around people. Her friends were out of town at college, and she felt abandoned. She texted them, but they hardly wanted to talk—always running to class or a party. She saw their smiling faces on Facebook and Instagram, but she hated seeing everyone so happy while she was so miserable. The doctors had given her something to quiet the ringing in her ears, but it was still there like the low hum of a refrigerator. Behind that, she couldn't hear much . . . barely audible mumbles and what sounded like low whispers.

She hated it. She'd rather be completely deaf than have these strange sounds cloud her thinking. She experimented with some music, letting it play as loudly as it would go in her earbuds, ignoring the popup message about "listening at high volumes . . . "

Damn phone! She could barely make out the music. It sounded monotone and lifeless, but it helped distract her ears from the ringing a little. She kept her earbuds in as she descended the stairs.

Her mother noticed the earbuds in Rebecca's ears and stopped . . . wondering what she could and couldn't hear. She decided not to pursue it yet. It was the first time in weeks she'd seen some life in her daughter, and, like a scared kitten, she didn't want to chase her away. Instead, she continued clearing the table and doing the dishes. She hummed a tune, hoping it would trigger something in Rebecca.

Rebecca walked straight to the fridge, opened it, and took out the milk. She put it on the table and turned to get a bowl. Her mother was standing there with the cereal and bowl in her hand extending it to Rebecca. She gasped, startled by the sudden appearance of her mother. Her mother stared at her with wide-eyes, and Rebecca realized that she must have gasped out loud.

She grabbed the bowl and cereal and put it on the table next to the milk. She was about to pour the cereal when she felt her cell phone buzz in her jeans pocket. She fished it out and clicked the rectangle button on the bottom to expose the text. She hoped it was a friend. She sure could use one about now.

Rebecca
Tell wht you do 2day

Nothing.
Just write normal, Mom . . . don't be cute.

Rebecca looked up at her mom, who sat across from her at the table.

I hate texting. We need to talk.

Why?

You need to learn to communicate.
Perhaps this is the best way for
now.

What do you mean "for now"?
You mean forever. I just want
to be with Tommy.

That's impossible. Tell me what
you want that isn't impossible.

It's not impossible to die, too.

Listen. Don't talk like
that. Quit feeling sorry for
yourself.

I can't listen. Have you forgotten?

She glared at her mother, who rolled her eyes.

> You know what I mean.

Rebecca poured her cereal and milk and began to eat.

> Leave me alone.

Never.

She wiped away the tears that filled her eyes.

Talk to me.

> I can't.

Well, then just read what I'm writing to you.

Rebecca nodded and took another bite of cereal . . . at least she wouldn't get yelled at for talking with her mouth full.

I called Dr. Talbot, and he's sending over a tutor . . . a college student to help you.

Rebecca leaned back in the chair after she'd read the text and glared at her mom. *How could she do that? How did anyone make house calls anymore?*

> I won't talk to him!

Rebecca warned, but her mother was gambling that she would. Rebecca pushed her food away and went back to her room.

CHAPTER 5

I don't know what to do. Mom wants me to see yet another doctor. She calls him a "tutor," but I know better. I've been poked and prodded to death. I'm sick of it. I'm beyond repair. They can't fix me. They should just throw me away.

And yet, I got my wish—I have silence. It's not complete—it's still like there's a buzzing refrigerator in my head—but at least it's a quiet one. Now if my other wish would come true: I wish the nightmares would stop. I keep seeing Tommy's eyes open . . . staring at me . . . bleeding. Oh God! Why did this have to happen to me? Why did you leave me so alone?!

A few days later, the tutor showed up on the front porch. His name was Michael Cartwright, and he looked a lot like Tommy to Rebecca. The short blond hair, the muscular body, and the blue—*no! They were brown! Just like mine*, Rebecca thought. She looked deep into his brown eyes as she shook his hand. Rebecca wanted to hug him, but she didn't dare. Instead, she clamped her heart shut.

Mary was surprised at how young Michael looked and how much he looked like Tommy. She hoped Rebecca would be all right with that. "He's young," Dr. Talbot had said, "but he's experienced and good at what he does. He might be just what Rebecca needs right now." Mary trusted the doctor and decided to give it a shot for Rebecca's sake.

Mrs. Kendall led Michael through the entryway up the front, dark-stained wooden stairs to the study, which was full of books on every wall and plants tucked into every corner. Rebecca called the study the "tropical rainforest."

The floors creaked slightly under their feet. Books lined the walls, and a large library table took up the middle of the room. A few padded brown desk chairs surrounded the table, and several lamps lit the area. It was cozy and not overly bright, even with the sun shining through the one window in the room. Two corners housed overstuffed chairs with signature upholstery and maroon pillows. Rebecca loved the study. She had spent many days and nights studying here, preparing for graduation and college. She pushed the thought of college out of her mind. Although she had planned on taking some time off between high school and college, she hadn't expected to spend it grieving.

"This is the study where you two will be working," Mary said as she signaled for Mike to sit down at the table. Rebecca chose the seat across from Mike, and Mary sat at the head of the table. "Tell us about yourself, Michael."

"Please, call me Mike. Well, I'm sure Dr. Talbot told you some things already. I'm a graduate student, and I teach people sign language and how to read lips. Dr. Talbot said that Rebecca needed help, so I hope I can help." He smiled at Rebecca while signing what he was saying.

Rebecca was mesmerized by his hands. They moved gracefully as he talked, and although she couldn't understand what he was saying, she felt comforted by his hand movements.

Mary handed Mike a slip of paper. "Here's Rebecca's cell number. We've been communicating via text. It seems easiest."

Mike took the slip of paper and nodded. "Okay. Sounds good." He started typing into his phone, and Rebecca's phone buzzed.

Hi, Becca. I'm Mike, and I'm here to help you learn sign language. Let's get started.

Rebecca was shocked. No one had called her Becca since she had been a child. Her father had called her that—not Jacob—but her birth father who had died just after her second birthday. Her mind held glimpses of him: Sam, her dad, so much like Tommy ... at least Tommy had been sober. She stopped spiraling into those thoughts of history repeating itself. She smiled at the memory but then frowned and fought back tears. She turned away briefly until she gathered her composure again.

Her mother left them alone so they could get acquainted. Rebecca wanted to tell him everything: about her dead father, her love for Tommy, her hopes and dreams. But she was afraid. *Later*, she thought.

Rebecca never knew she could learn so much in just one hour. She found out that he loved cars and drove a new Camaro Convertible—Rebecca's dream car. Originally from California, he moved to Flagstaff to attend NAU for the master's program. He had attended college and high school at the same time and graduated from UCLA the previous year. He loved boats, horses, tigers, music, and skiing. She also learned the alphabet in American Sign Language. Her hands were tired after spelling everything.

Mike couldn't think of another day when he had learned absolutely nothing about a person. All he knew about Rebecca was that she was 19. She had blondish-brown hair, brown eyes, and her boyfriend was killed in an accident. Hobbies—it was hobbies he wanted to find out about. He had hoped that by giving her a nickname right away she would feel more comfortable. He had guessed at Becca rather than Becky, but it hadn't really worked. Her faded look and frown confused him. He decided to keep trying. *There's always tomorrow*, he thought.

The next day, Mike wanted to get Becca to talk out loud. He thought that he could help draw her out of her shell.

In the study, he started right away by texting her.

Have you tried talking out loud?

No I haven't.

But she had lied. She had tried in the privacy of her bathroom, but she was afraid of how she might sound. She didn't want him to hear her.

Then try, please.

Rebecca looked blankly at Mike. She shook her head.

Becca, you need to try. You can do it.

She opened her mouth and uttered a sound. Mike encouraged her with his hands, and he leaned toward her across the desk.

Rebecca shook her head again, and her face turned red.

Mike got up and moved to the chair at the head of the table. They'd been sitting across the table from each other, but it was time to close the gap.

He scooted closer to her. She turned her chair to face his, and he took her hands. They were cold, and he briefly rubbed them to warm them.

"You can do this," he said.

Rebecca could tell what he was saying by his facial expressions. When he touched her hands, a spark went through her. Somehow, she wanted to please Mike. She also wanted to talk to him. There was so much to say!

Rebecca's eyes were wide, but she licked her lips and spouted out a slew of words. Words came out, but they weren't comprehensible to Mike. He only heard whispered mumbles, but it encouraged him to keep pushing her.

Mike smiled. "Yes! Now, feel the words," Mike said and pointed to his mouth. "Feel them in your mouth."

Becca looked confused, so Mike typed it in his phone, dropping her hands back into her lap. She leaned back in the chair as she read his text and then responded.

I'll try. What should I say?

Start with your name.

Rebecca opened her mouth and thought of each letter and tried to feel them in her mouth before she spoke. "R-E-B-E-C-C-A."

Mike smiled, nodded encouragement, and took her hands again.

Rebecca added all of her names the next time: "R-E-B-E-C-C-A-C-A-D-E-N-C-E-K-E-N-D-A-L-L." She said it over and over. She could feel the words in her mouth and throat. She also thought she heard herself but was unsure with the ringing and muffled tones in her ears.

Mike couldn't get over her voice. She sounded fantastic! Maybe he was a bit biased because he knew she hadn't spoken in weeks. It wasn't perfect, but after only two days, she was progressing. He had reached out to her and gotten a response, but her expression still held a sense of suspicion and anger. He hoped he could break her shell even just a little bit. Next time, he would try something else.

♪♪♪

I like that Mike called me "Becca" but I wonder if I should ask him to stop. I think of Dad . . . Sam . . . I don't even know what to call him. I forget about him sometimes, and yet, there's a gentle place in my heart for him. When I think about him, I don't grieve. I grieve for Tommy, and then I think of the parallels between him and Sam, and I want to scream. Why did God do this to me? Why? But I have to move on . . . I can't let this grief cripple me. I must find a way.

The next day, Mike asked Rebecca a simple question in text:

Tell me something about tomorrow.

Rebecca took her time in her response. She wanted it to come out perfectly.

> Tomorrow never comes; it turns
> into today, then into yesterday, etc.
> There is no tomorrow, only today.
> Yet, today never stays the same.
> That's why we call it the present,
> but soon that turns to the past. I
> could go on and on, but I won't.
> So, that's what I think of tomorrow;
> it's never really there.

Mike hesitated. He hadn't really meant to get a philosophical response but was happy she was responding to him. He decided to keep her attention. He began to speak slowly so she could try reading his lips. "Read my lips," he said, pointing to his lips.

"O.K." Rebecca replied in sign language.

"Tell me something about the present."

Rebecca looked confused. "P-R-E-S-E-N-T" she spelled with her hands, tilting her head to indicate the question. Mike nodded.

> You mean like today?

Mike nodded.

Rebecca thought for a moment and then she smiled.

> I suppose the present is a gift to
> learn. It turns to the past, yet you
> still have the present. It's time
> and very confusing. Why are you
> asking these things?

I want to learn more about you.

Rebecca smiled and looked into Mike's eyes. He turned away and sat up in his chair.

When he had come in that day, he immediately sat in the chair next to her. They conversed facing each other, but now he moved back across the table.

They reviewed the alphabet in sign language and he spoke each letter, asking her to do the same. She did. She continued to work with him but was confused by his sudden distance.

After Mike left, Rebecca sat in the study for a while. She heard a song. It was impossible, but she closed her eyes and listened. It was in her mind. It had to be. Where else was it? She listened; there were no words, just music. A song that didn't even exist. She wished she could go to the piano and pick it out. Instead, she went to her room and cried.

CHAPTER 6

*A dream. Dreams give us a point in life.
Something to remember in a time of need.
A dream. What is my dream? My dream–a
dream, impossible to fulfill now. A dream
with love and music. I want to sing and let
the world know how I feel. I don't want to
be a rock star but a . . .*

She was interrupted by a tap on the shoulder. She turned around to face her mother.

It had been months since Rebecca and Mike started working together. She had progressed quite a bit. She could read lips and sign more than just the alphabet. Even her parents had learned sign language! She had learned how to read lips so well that her parents sometimes forgot she was deaf. They would turn away, and Rebecca would have to remind them to turn toward her when they spoke. Rebecca continued her tutoring with Mike, but she wanted to get out of the house and do something else. She longed for her friends and her old life of parties and music. With the help of her psychiatrist, Dr. Ryan, and Mike, she wasn't as depressed as she had been, but she still felt lonely.

"Rebecca," her mom signed as she picked up Rebecca's shoes from the middle of the floor and put them in the closet. "You got mail." She handed her a thick, pink envelope.

"Happy Birthday, sweetie," she said and left the room.

"Thank you," Rebecca signed and ripped open the envelope.

It was from her best friend—Christy Taylor. They had been friends since seventh grade. They were extremely close and extreme opposites. Christy had dark brown skin and black hair. She was tall and skinny. She had a happy-go-lucky personality, which Rebecca was sometimes jealous of.

The card was cheesy and had pink and gold butterflies all over it, but she loved it! Surrounding the gold embossed "Happy Birthday," Christy had written a note in different colored pens:

Hey, Birthday Girl! I sent you a card! I thought I'd try this old-fashioned thing for once. I hope you have a happy birthday. I'm sorry I wasn't there for you during everything. I didn't even get home for Christmas! But I'll be home this summer. Promise! Hang in there!

Love,
Christy

She went out on the balcony and continued to write:

> *I can't believe it's March 10th already! I forgot my own birthday! I think everyone else forgot, too. I'm surprised Stefan didn't even remember. At least I got a card in the mail from Christy—an old-fashioned card through snail mail, even! Wow! She says she'll be home this summer. I can't wait!! I was kind of mad at her for not being around even at Christmas, but I guess these things happen. I was worried we weren't friends anymore. All I saw were her pictures on Instagram and Facebook. She's having a great time at Washington State. I wish I were there with her. I don't know why I decided to wait a year. We could've been there together. Oh well . . . Can't change the past. I'm not even sure I want to go to college now. All I want's a song. That's my dream, and I'm not even sure how it can come true now. How am I supposed to sing when I can't hear? It breaks my heart.*

She closed her notebook and her eyes and felt the March sun on her face. She wanted to write down the poem spinning in her head, but she couldn't get it out.

Her parents hadn't forgotten about her birthday, though. Her mom fixed her favorite dinner, Cornish game hens with asparagus, and she opened her presents. Her parents had gotten her a smart watch so she could read her texts on her wrist without holding her phone all the time. It also had vibrating notifications. They also gave her a tablet for her writing and studying. In the end, her birthday wasn't so bad.

The next day, although it was Sunday, Mike came by with a birthday present. The wrapping paper was blue, and it sparkled. It had a little silver bow on the top. It was a small, square package. "Well, aren't you going to open it?"

Rebecca held it in her hands; the poem in her mind began to take shape. She opened the package and found a little velvet box. She opened that and found a silver necklace that sparkled in the dimly lit room. A heart dangled from the chain as Mike took it out of the box and put it around Rebecca's neck. He stepped back to admire it.

"I love it," Rebecca said as she gave Mike a hug.

Her mother walked in just as Rebecca gave Mike his hug.

"So that's what goes on in the study?"

"No, it's not," Mike said. Mike began to explain, but Rebecca interrupted, not realizing it.

"Look at my birthday present, Mom!" She showed her mother the heart dangling on her neck. "Isn't it lovely?"

"Yes, it is. So, that's why you were hugging him?"

"Of course! You didn't think anything did you?"

"Oh, of course not!"

Mike began to laugh and then gathered his things. "I've got to go," he said.

Mike said goodbye to Rebecca and then left.

"Oh, Rebecca," her mother began. "What I came up here to say was that another birthday present is at the airport,"

"Well, what's it doing there? Let's go get it!"

Rebecca rushed to her room and grabbed her notebook. The poem spun in her head. Her mother gathered up her husband, and they headed for the door. "What's the ruckus about?" Jacob asked.

"Never mind. Get into the car. We're driving to the airport!" Mary opened the door and playfully shoved Mr. Kendall out the door.

Rebecca climbed into the back of the car and opened her notebook to a poem she had started a long time ago.

"Why are we going to the airport?" Jacob asked Mary.

She moved into a position where Rebecca couldn't read her lips. "Stefan is at the airport, and we're picking him up. He couldn't get here yesterday, so he's here today. After that, we're going to church."

"What? Church? We're not church people!" Mary rolled her eyes at the old joke. Of course they were church people. They went almost every Sunday, and Rebecca used to sing in the choir. Now . . . well, now they just went once in a while without Rebecca.

Rebecca read the little poem she began when she started seeing Dr.Ryan:

I'm missing you.
There are some things I'm missing,
Mostly I'm missing you.
I miss the birds and the noise they make,

Mostly I'm missing you.
Time has gone by for my heart to mend
Time has gone by for me to meet a friend.
I met a guy today, and he might just sweep me away.

Rebecca thought for a moment about the last line. *Oh yeah. Now I remember*, she thought. *I wrote the last line when I met Michael.* She began to write, feeling the memory as the words in her mind spilled out.

He has become my friend,
More and more each day.
The pain in my heart is not much, anymore.
I've finally learned to open up the door.
So, goodbye, my friend,
I'm afraid this is the end.
You are only a memory
But that lasts for much more
Than love.

It wasn't the greatest, but it would have to do. All she needed was a melody. It was there; she could feel it, but it just wasn't right. Not for those words.

They finally arrived at the airport. Jacob looked at the airport screens to see if the flight was arriving on time. They strolled to the baggage claim area.

They sat at the tiny baggage claim department at the Flagstaff Airport and waited for the conveyor belt to start moving. It seemed like hours before passengers began to file into the area. Mary missed the days when people could meet passengers at the gate.

She thought she saw Stefan approaching her, but she convinced herself it was her imagination.

"Hi, Rebecca," he said.

"It is Stefan!" Rebecca said out loud. She gave him a hug, almost strangling him.

Stefan had been her friend in high school but had graduated a year before her and joined the Navy right after graduation. Rebecca hadn't seen him since. She followed him on Facebook and messaged him from time-to-time, but he had been sequestered while going through training. It was good to finally see him—red hair and all.

"It's nice to be home!" he yelped as he picked up Rebecca in his arms and swung her around.

"Well, you aren't quite home yet," Mrs. Kendall reminded him. "We're grateful your mom let us pick you up. We'd better get you back to her. Then we're all going out to dinner and church."

"Sounds good to me," he said and put his arm around Rebecca's neck. They headed for the car while Stefan told story after story. Rebecca had a hard time understanding what he was saying because he would only face her once in a while. She didn't mind, though. It was good just to have him near. Finally, after two years, she was with her friend again.

That evening, after going out to dinner, the family went to church with Stefan and his mom. Rebecca hadn't been to church since before the accident and wondered why her parents had decided to go.

♫♫♫

Rebecca was surprised to see Mike at church. "Hi!" she said as she approached him with Stefan behind her.

"Oh, hi! How are you?" he asked.

"Oh, great. I want you to meet my friend, Stefan."

"Hi!" Stefan stepped forward, and they shook hands.

Rebecca had told Mike about Stefan, and he knew they were just friends, but he couldn't help feel a little jealous.

"So, how do you know Rebecca?" Stefan asked.

"Well, I've been her tutor since her accident."

"I'm glad you were there for her. I've been training on an island in the Indian Ocean. No Facebook. No real cell service . . . nothin'. I feel like I've been on a deserted island! I'm so far behind in everyone's life!"

"You were on a deserted island?" Rebecca asked, misunderstanding Stefan.

Stefan shook his head. "I FEEL like it," he said with his hand on the small of Rebecca's back.

Rebecca smiled at Mike and Stefan and then joined her parents who went to sit close to the front near Stefan's mom.

Stefan turned back to Mike. "I'm in the Navy—survival training," he whispered. "Tell me more about yourself. Where are you from?"

"I'm from California, but you don't wanna hear my life story just before church. Let's get together sometime."

"Sounds like a plan," Stefan said and shook Mike's hand again, squeezing it until he felt Mike's knuckles pop.

Mike headed to his seat shaking his hand in pain from Stefan's handshake.

The preacher entered, and the sermon opened with one of Rebecca's favorite hymns. They stood and the music began. Rebecca sang the words in her mind as the congregation sang. Her mother glanced at her.

"You know the words," she signed, "you've sung it a thousand times." Rebecca looked down at the words; Stefan showed her where they were.

Rebecca began to sing quietly, barely whispering the words. Her mother nodded, letting her know she had the right key. Rebecca sang louder, feeling the words and the notes. Although she couldn't hear the congregation, she knew the song so well that she could hear it in her mind. Just like she had been taught to sing, she thought the note and then sang it. The only difference was she couldn't hear it. Instead, she felt like her ears were plugged, and everything was muffled.

Mike, who was sitting in front of them, heard Becca singing. He didn't dare turn around, afraid that it would silence her. Instead, he smiled and felt a surge of emotion. Her voice, although timid, sounded pure. He wanted to listen to her sing all day, but the song ended, and they sat down.

Rebecca beamed. *I can sing! I can sing!* But then the thought occurred to her that maybe they were just being nice. *How do I know if I can really sing. I can't hear myself, so how do I know?*

Mrs. Kendall talked to the preacher and told him that Rebecca had sung all the hymns.

"Well, that's good," he said. He knew what had happened, and he tried to encourage Rebecca as much as he could.

After church, Mike was invited for Sunday game night. He accepted the invitation.

When they got to Rebecca's house, Stefan and Mike went into the study to talk.

After some small talk, Stefan asked, "So, how do you think Rebecca is handling things? I worry about her, ya know."

Without revealing too much, Mike answered, "It's been hard, but I think she's getting used to the idea."

"She seems different: more reserved, quiet."

"I'm not surprised," Mike said. "An accident like that will change a person. What concerns me, though, is that she doesn't think of the future. It's now or yesterday, but never tomorrow. I try to get her to talk about what she wants to do as a career or even where she wants to go to college. She starts to tell me, but then she clams up and never says another word."

"So, she hasn't told you her dream?" he asked, surprised.

"No. I don't even know her favorite color. What does she like to do?"

"She loves to sing—ever since she found out she could." He remembered the time that Rebecca told him one day after school. It had been a bad day at school for him. He'd failed a math test and faced having to tell his mother. As a single mom, she wanted more for Stefan than she could ever give. That's why he joined the Navy. He wanted to go to college to be an engineer, and he knew his mother could never afford it. So, he joined up, not really understanding what it meant at the time. Now he knew, and he liked the discipline of it. He took the Navy track, and they trained him for engineering. In a few more years, he'd get out and go to college on their dime. It seemed a perfect plan.

"I have to tell you a secret," Rebecca had whispered, pulling him closer. She had looked around as if checking to make sure there were no listening drones or cameras. They stopped in the middle of the sidewalk, and Rebecca whispered in his ear, "I have a dream—a purpose in life. I want to sing."

"You want to be a singer?" he asked, looking down at her. When he looked down, he must have sneered. She looked crushed. Quickly, he smiled. "That's great, Rebecca! You want to be a singer, I want to be an engineer, and now we know where we're headed in life." He'd almost kissed her, but she pulled away. Stefan left that part out of the story.

She began walking again with a dreamy look in her eye. "Not just a singer. Someone special. A songwriter, too. I just want to let the world know how I feel."

"I understand. I'll help you fulfill that dream."

"Ah, you're the greatest friend I could have!" She hugged him, and Stefan sighed . . . stuck in the friend zone.

"Why a secret?" he'd asked Rebecca.

"Because people would laugh. I don't want anyone to know it's my dream 'til it comes true."

She had sworn him to secrecy, and although he didn't understand why, he hadn't told anyone until now.

"I knew she wasn't kidding," Stefan said to Mike. "Don't let her know I told you. She would never forgive me."

"I won't. Thanks for telling me. That helps a lot."

"One more thing. Part of her dream has come true. She's someone special."

"Yeah, I know. When you work with someone as special as she is, you get attached."

"You're right, but do me a favor. Don't hurt her."

Mike looked at Stefan's serious gaze and nodded. "I promise," he said, worried he had revealed too much.

"Good, now let's go play some games."

"Sounds great." They left the study laughing and in good spirits.

"Came down just in time," Mrs. Kendall said as she put the Yatzhee game on the dining room table next to her famous game-night spread of chips, nuts, dips, and chocolates.

"It's game time!" she hollered, hoping everyone would come running. Mary missed having people over for game night. With just the three of them lately, she longed for the times when Rebecca would invite Stefan, Christy, and her other friends after evening church services.

Of course, Rebecca hadn't heard her mother, but she came out of the living room, looking at her phone. She wanted to take a picture and let everyone on Facebook see their smiling faces. Stefan had the worst luck and never won any of the games they played, but he was always a good sport about it. As she was typing her post, she ran right into Mike, who was on his way from the dining room to let her know it was time to start.

"Oh, I'm sorry," she said as she looked into Mike's brown eyes.

"Don't worry about it," he smiled at Rebecca and put his hands on her arms. "What are you reading?"

"I'm posting on Facebook. Christy will be so jealous that she's missing out. But that's what she gets for goin' to an out-of-state college."

"Rebecca, you know the rule: no phones at the table for game night! Now put it away and sit down," Mrs. Kendall said. Mike had to relay the message because Rebecca didn't see Mrs. Kendall's lips. She was still looking into Mike's brown eyes.

"Have a seat," Mike said as he pulled out a chair for Rebecca.

"Thank you." She put her phone away and sat down. Stefan and Jacob came out of the kitchen laughing. Stefan's mom had decided not to stay, so it was the five of them.

"Okay. Each of you get a die to roll to see who goes first." Mary passed around the cup with the dice as Rebecca stared at her. "What is wrong, Rebecca?" she signed.

"It's like the good ol' days," Rebecca signed back and smiled.

"Hey!" Stefan said. "No cheating! You know I don't know sign language. Ya guys are gonna have to speak from here on out!"

Rebecca and her mom smiled at each other. They hadn't always been close, but this experience had brought them closer, and they had spent many hours studying sign language together. They had even practiced signing poems and songs back and forth trying to understand. It had been effective. Now, they were nearly masters and closer than before.

As they played, the five of them laughed and tossed the dice on the table. As usual, Stefan lost. Since there was another person playing, Rebecca thought Stefan had a chance, but Mike won two of the six games they played. It was getting late, but Rebecca didn't want it to end yet.

"Look. It's like 8 and still light out," Stefan said.

"Yup, you've forgotten it's almost spring. The days are finally getting longer!" Mrs. Kendall answered.

"Rebecca, you want to get some fresh air?" Mike signed as Mrs. Kendall cleared off the table.

"Sure," she said. They started towards the door.

"Leaving already?" Stefan asked Mike.

"No. We're going to get some fresh air," Mike explained.

"Sounds like a good idea," he said. He led the way out as Mike and Rebecca looked at each other in disbelief. They followed him and sat on the porch steps.

"One thing about early spring: no mosquitoes," Stefan said as he sat between Mike and Rebecca. Mike turned so Rebecca couldn't read his lips.

"I said I wouldn't hurt her," he said.

"Yeah, I know, but I'm not sure I want to let her go," he answered practically whispering.

"I don't blame you. But, you might have to." Mike glared at Stefan.

"What's all the talking about? I can't read your lips when you're turned like that," Rebecca said as she grabbed Stefan's shirt sleeve. "No secrets!"

"No secrets!" Stefan said with both hands up in surrender. "Why was your hearing loss kept a secret? All I knew was that you were in an accident. Then I come home and you're using sign language and not singing! From anyone else I can understand, but from your best friend?" Rebecca looked down at the grass. Her eyes filled with tears.

Then she looked up, her eyes getting hard, "Don't yell at me! What? Am I supposed to post it on Facebook? Hey world: I'm deaf!! Don't yell at me! Just because I can't hear my favorite song or the birds!"

Stefan got up and started to leave. Her eyes softened. She got up and took Stefan's hands in hers. "I didn't want you to treat me differently. We've been friends forever, and I was afraid you'd stop loving me. I was also afraid you'd just feel sorry for me. I love you, Stefan." She gave him a hug. She looked over his shoulder and saw Mike walking away. She stopped hugging Stefan and looked him straight in the eye.

"I'll help you fulfill your dream," he said.

"I know it's our secret, but now I want to share it," she answered.

Stefan nodded and closed his eyes. *Still stuck in the friend zone*, he thought.

Rebecca turned back and ran toward Mike, who was crossing the street. His car sparkled in the street light. As he reached for the door handle, Rebecca caught up with him. "Why are you leaving," she asked, and he turned around to face her.

"You guys were having an intense conversation. I felt like an intruder. I thought you two should talk," Mike said, looking at her, his hand on his car door handle.

"We did. But I want to talk to you, now."

"Okay. You wanna go for a ride?" He stopped and waited for her to answer.

Rebecca looked up at the darkening sky. "It's getting dark. I'd rather walk."

Mike laughed a little and then saw the fear in Rebecca's eyes. "Okay, I understand." They began to walk, Mike on the outside and Rebecca on the inside.

"I haven't been telling you everything I should be telling you," Rebecca said after they had been walking for a while in silence.

"Oh yeah?" Mike answered.

"I used to be able to talk about the future more than the past. That's changed in a way I can't express."

"I understand."

"I have a dream, a dream that only Stefan knows about." They stopped. Rebecca looked deep into Mike's eyes. "I want you to know, too, and that means you're somebody special."

Mike looked up at the sky; the clouds were clearing and turning pink. A few stars started to peek out one by one. He felt like he was falling "in love," but he was trying to fight it. She was young and had her whole life ahead of her. "Tell me your dream," he said as he came back to earth and took her hands.

"I want to sing. I don't want to be a rock star or a pop star, but I want to be someone special. I want to let the world know how I feel about things. I want to write songs . . . simple songs."

"You are someone special. There's something I don't understand, though. If you want to let the world know how you feel about things, why don't you let me know?"

She nodded and looked at the ground before answering. "I've changed since the accident, Mike, but I can't let myself do that. I'm bottled up inside. I'm afraid to . . . "

"Afraid of what?"

"Afraid of myself. I'm afraid of what I can't do."

"What can't you do?"

"Sing." She turned and began to walk away.

"Rebecca!" Mike yelled. Of course, she couldn't hear him. He let her go. She needed to be alone. He watched her cross the street and break out into a run. She was heading for the park. Mike watched her 'til she was out of sight. Slowly, he turned back toward the house.

Rebecca ran until sweat poured down her face. She turned at the park and sat on the swings and pushed herself back and forth with her feet. She breathed heavily in the blackening night. The sun had gone down; it was hard to see without the park lights. Finally, they came on, and Rebecca stared at her shadow. Soon, she saw another one. She looked up and saw Stefan standing there. She stopped her swinging, and he knelt in front of her. The lights shimmered in his eyes. "Are you okay?" he asked. "You must be depressed. I haven't seen you run that hard for a long time."

"I'm okay. You want to walk me home?"

"Sure." Rebecca got up, and they walked toward her house.

CHAPTER 7

I can't hear the children play
But the thing is . . .
I feel my heart beat fast for you
I can't hear the beginning of each day
I can't hear the new birds singing
But the thing is . . .
I see and feel much for you.

That was all she could write. *The rest will come later*, she thought. A melody ran in her head, but she blocked it out. It was right for those words, but she wanted to wait until it was done.

The next day, Mike arrived a little late to Rebecca's. He'd been stuck on the phone discussing some old business in California.

"Hi," he said. Rebecca was sitting at the desk with her feet propped up and her tablet on her lap.

She looked up and then back to her tablet. "Hi," she answered and continued working on her tablet.

"Look," he said, but she did not look up. He sighed and kneeled before her, forcing her to look at him. "We're going on a field trip."

Rebecca looked shocked. "What? Why?" she asked.

"Just come with me, please." He held out his hand, and she took it, putting her tablet on the desk. "Bring it," he said.

"Okay," she answered and grabbed her backpack and tablet.

In his metallic blue Camaro, Rebecca stared at the computer screen on the dashboard. "Nice car," she said as Mike climbed into the driver's seat.

"Thanks," he said. "Rear camera, digital readout, satellite radio, heated seats." He smiled at Rebecca as the silver leather seat started to warm.

"What are all the dials for?"

"Tire pressure. Air conditioning. Oil. Gas. It also has Bluetooth to connect to my cell phone."

Rebecca smiled and nodded. "Cool," she said.

They left the parking spot in front of the house, and Rebecca leaned against the door as she watched Mike speak and sign with one hand. "Have you written any poems?" he asked.

"Yeah, a lot. The last one sucks."

"I'd like to hear it sometime."

"Okay, but you won't like it." Rebecca turned away from Mike and watched the houses speed by as they drove to the NAU campus.

The car stopped in front of the music building on campus, and Mike said, "Here we are!"

"How many floors does this building have?" Rebecca asked as she entered the elevator.

Mike showed her the buttons and pressed "B" for the basement. "Yeah, but of course it's no where near as many as the Empire State Building." Mike was talking to himself because Rebecca was trying to understand what the guy next to her was saying. The doors opened, and Mike pulled Rebecca out of the elevator. The guy stumbled out also.

"Can I buy you a drink?" he asked Rebecca.

"She's with me," Mike interrupted. He pulled Rebecca away before the man could reply. "You have to watch out for these weirdos." He opened what looked like an office door. Rebecca entered and saw a big man look down at her with his hands on his hips. He was about to kick her out, but he smiled when he saw Mike.

"Well, why didn't you say you were with him? Hi, I'm Burt."

He extended his hand, and Rebecca cautiously shook it.

"Hi, Burt!" Mike said as he brushed by him, "Where's Monty?"

"Oh, he's in the back. Who's your lady friend?" He let go of Rebecca's hand and turned away from her to face Mike.

"That's Becca." He brushed past Burt again and took Rebecca's hand and led her through a door to the right. She expected to enter a regular office, but it was a unique room with music posters hanging from the ceiling, carpet on the walls, and a desk in the middle of the room.

A man sat at the desk with his back toward the door. "Monty," Mike said. The man turned around and frowned at Mike.

"Don't you know how to knock?" he asked putting his phone on the desk and standing up.

"Sure, but I didn't want to have to make an appointment at the front desk." The two men shook hands, and Monty pointed to Rebecca.

"Who are you?" he asked.

"That's Becca. She's what I want to talk about."

"Okay, let's go talk." He opened up a door to the room Mike and Rebecca had just left.

"Rebecca, get acquainted with Burt. He's a nice guy," Monty said holding the door open.

"Do I have to?" she signed to Mike.

"You don't have to, but it's better if you do," he said and smiled.

Rebecca nodded and entered the room.

The control room, which seemed to be a long hallway, held a myriad of equipment: a desk with a computer, knobs, and levers. Burt sat at the controls and typed on the keyboard. Above him, a large window looked into a large recording studio full of instruments and microphones. To her right, Rebecca saw a door and opened it. It led her into the recording room. Guitars lined the back wall and a drum set occupied a corner.

Rebecca walked to the back of the room and picked out an acoustic guitar. She sat on the stool in the center of the room and began to play a few chords . . . the few chords she knew. She had no idea if the guitar was in tune or not, but she knew the chords she was playing, and she heard the song in her head, even if she didn't hear the notes she played.

Scowling, Mike walked out of Monty's office. He saw Rebecca playing the guitar and turned around.

Rebecca began to play her favorite gospel song, and she sang along quietly.

"Listen," Mike said to Monty as he pulled him out of his office. Monty rolled his eyes but flipped a switch on the control panel and listened. Rebecca's voice filled the little room. It was sweet and quiet.

And Jesus said, "Come to the water stand by my side
I know you are thirsty you won't be denied.
I felt every tear drop where in darkness you cried
And I strove to remind you that for those tears I died.

She continued with the verses, not knowing that Mike, Monty, and Burt were listening.

"Isn't she great?" Mike asked.

"I don't know," Monty answered.

"She's good, boss," Burt interrupted. Monty flipped the switch again. Rebecca's voice faded.

"I'm not asking you to like it. Just record it."

"Nope, I won't do that. She's deaf! She'll be impossible to work with," Monty said. He turned to go into his office, but Mike stopped him.

"That didn't stop me from loving her. It shouldn't stop you from recording her." Monty pulled away and slammed the door.

"She's deaf?" Burt asked.

"Yeah," Mike answered as he watched Rebecca put the guitar away.

"No wonder she didn't answer my questions."

Rebecca opened the door and saw Mike smiling at her.

"Was it that bad?" she asked. Mike laughed and shook his head.

"I didn't know you played guitar."

She told him about how Jacob had taught her a few chords and how to play a few songs. "That song, and 'Learning to Fly' are the ones I know the best. I really can't play much beyond that without music."

"I'm impressed," he said. He put his arm around Rebecca, and they left the studio. "You can really sing."

When they reached his car, Mike started the engine and then pointed to the screen on his dashboard.

"Look," he said, and she watched the screen. It glowed silver and a green arrow moved up and down. It reminded her of a heart monitor at the hospital, but this had less of a solid pattern. Then the image switched to a half circle with lines and tick marks. The center marks were green, and the marks around it were gray blue. When Mike made a sound, a needle moved to the left or the right.

"That's a tuner, Mike," Rebecca said. "I used to use one when I tuned my guitar, but I rarely needed it. I could hear the notes and know whether or not it was in tune. How are you doing that?"

"That's exactly what it is," Mike said. "It's an app on my phone. So, sing an 'A'."

Rebecca looked at him, skeptical. "What? Just sing an 'A'? Just like that?"

Mike nodded.

Rebecca rolled her eyes but opened her mouth and sang what she thought was an 'A'. The needle wobbled back and forth. In her head, she could hear the 'A', but from her voice, she heard nothing. She had no idea whether she was in key or not. But the tuner showed her that she was close. From there, she didn't know what to do.

"Feel the note in your throat?" Mike asked.

Rebecca concentrated. She wasn't sure. She pushed more air out of her mouth, and the needle jumped up. She was sharp. She adjusted her tongue and throat, and the needle went nearly to "0." It still wobbled back and forth, but the needle stayed in the green zone until she ran out of air.

"So, I'm singing in tune?!" she asked.

Mike nodded, and they grinned together.

Mike tapped her on the shoulder. He signed, "Are you hungry?"

Rebecca nodded at him and continued playing with the tuner app.

They left campus and drove to a restaurant for lunch.

As Rebecca munched on a French fry, she asked, "What did you say to Monty?"

"I asked him if you could sing with the band," he answered taking a sip of iced tea. "He said that he would have to hear you first. I walked out and saw you playing the guitar and singing, so I told him to listen." Mike stopped to let Rebecca speak, but she closed her mouth and waited for him to continue. "So, he listened, but not really. I liked it. So did Burt. You can sure sing, though."

"Yeah, maybe," Rebecca answered with a smile.

"I told him he didn't need to like it, just record it. Then he gave me some lame excuse about your being deaf. He was worried about the logistics—singing with the band, etc."

"You told him?" Rebecca looked surprised.

"Not everything,"

"But still!"

"I'm sorry, but I had to," Mike responded.

Rebecca looked at the floor, then looked up. "I suppose you let it go with that!?"

"No, I didn't!"

"What did you tell him?"

He wiped his hands on his napkin and looked at Rebecca's brown eyes. "I told him that . . . it shouldn't matter . . . and that I loved you, and why couldn't he record your song anyway."

Rebecca looked stunned and switched to sign language, "You told him that you loved me?"

"Yes, I did."

"But . . . do you?"

"Yes, I do."

"How . . . ?"

"Don't ask me questions. All I know is that you're someone special, and I think I love you."

"Think?"

"It doesn't matter anyway. I'm not really free to make my own decisions."

"What is that supposed to mean?"

"I can't explain. Not now. Can we talk about it later?"

"No," Rebecca signed, "Let's talk about it now."

Mike looked at the people watching them from the neighboring table and sighed. "No. Let me take you home. We'll talk about it later."

Rebecca pushed away her plate and nodded.

Mike fidgeted with the check and paid it with his card. They left the restaurant and drove to Rebecca's house in silence.

In front of Rebecca's house, she started to get out of the car, but Mike stopped her with his hand on her arm. She turned towards him, and he started to talk.

"Becca, I have to let you go," he said.

Rebecca looked surprised. "What?" she asked.

"I'm turning you over to another tutor," he said.

Rebecca shook her head and looked out the window. It was late, but she could see the trees wavering in the wind.

"Why are you leaving now?"

"I need to get back to California." He toyed with his keys and then looked her in the eye. "I have some things to take care of there."

"But what about school?"

"Spring Break is coming up, and I've made arrangements with the professors to get my stuff in afterward."

Rebecca looked at Mike. "I want you to stay, not just because you're a good tutor but because I like you."

Mike put his hand on her shoulder, "I like you, too, but you're my client and it wouldn't be right."

"But you said you loved me. How can you say that and then just leave?"

Mike leaned back and smoothed his hair back. "There's so much you don't understand."

"Then tell me," she said.

Mike looked out the window and shook his head. "I can't," he signed.

Rebecca shook her head and wiped a tear from her eye and pursed her lips. "Okay, have it your way," she said and climbed out of the car.

The wind had picked up, and Rebecca brushed her hair behind her ears. Strands stuck to the tears on her face as she ran to the front door. She fiddled with the lock until the door finally opened.

Much like her mood, the house was dark and empty. She checked her phone, but her mother hadn't texted or called. She sent a text to her mom.

Where are you?

But there wasn't an immediate response. With nothing left to do, Rebecca stood on the patio attached to her room and let the wind blow the tears from her eyes.

CHAPTER 8

Her smartwatch notification interrupted Rebecca's reverie. It was a text from her mom.

> We're at the hospital with Stefan and his mom.
>
> We're O.K., but Stefan's mom is not good. Be home when we can.

Without a car, Rebecca was left to worry about Stefan and his mom. She texted her mom, but there was no response. She tried to work on her song, but to no avail. Finally, at midnight, the front door opened, and in walked her parents and a distraught Stefan.

She ran to him and held him. His head bent in grief on her shoulder. "What happened?" she mouthed to her mom.

Mary started signing the events but was at a loss for the sign for "unconscious" and "dead." She shrugged mid-sign and then signaled for Rebecca to ask Stefan.

He had arrived home that evening after hanging out with his friends to find his mother passed out in the middle of the kitchen floor. He called 911 after feeling for a pulse. They arrived, but it had been too late. She'd had a brain aneurism. She had died on her kitchen floor.

"I'm so sorry," Rebecca said.

"I'll fix up the guest room for you, Stefan," Mary said. "You can stay as long as you like." She ascended the stairs with Jacob as he went to help her tidy the room and prepare for a long-term guest.

Stefan and Rebecca moved to the couch by the picture window. Between sobs, Stefan relayed the events of the night. Rebecca couldn't understand everything as he cried and talked, but she let him talk, releasing the grief like a faucet.

"I can't believe she's gone," Stefan said after several minutes. Rebecca held him close, tears in her own eyes.

"I remember spending so many nights at your house while she made popcorn and watched scary movies with us. It was like she was my mom, too." Rebecca remembered the tiny woman who had a constant smile on her lips and kind words for everyone she met. The night seemed unreal. Grief stricken, Rebecca stared at Stefan.

He stroked her hair and looked into her moist eyes. "You loved her, too," he said. Rebecca nodded.

Then Stefan leaned in and kissed her . . . his lips were soft on hers and a little salty from his tears. She kissed him back, lost in the moment, but then she pulled back, putting her hand on his chest. "Stefan," she whispered. "It's late. You're tired. Get some sleep."

She stood up from the couch and put her hand out for him. He took it, and she led him up the stairs to the guest room where her mother finished putting the green sheets on the double bed. It was as if she were leading a child . . . the Navy man was long gone, and what was left was a shell.

CHAPTER 9

A kiss. A first kiss. I can't believe Stefan kissed me. It's crazy! It was nice, but he's my friend. I don't think I could ever think of him as more than that. And yet . . . I liked his kiss. I can't believe Linda is gone. She had been like a second mom to me. We all spent so much time together, we were like family. My head is reeling! How can so much have happened in one day?

Rebecca shook her head and scratched out the words. The night before was a blur to Rebecca, and the next day, it all seemed unreal. She clung to her routine and went downstairs to help her mother with breakfast.

Later, Rebecca tapped on the door to Stefan's room. She held a tray with eggs, bacon, and orange juice.

"Stefan, it's Rebecca. I have breakfast. You'll have to open the door."

Stefan, red hair disheveled and shirt off, opened the door. "I'll come down," Stefan said as he took the tray.

"You better put a shirt on, though." Rebecca licked her lips. She had never noticed the chiseled body under the Navy uniform before. Last night's kiss returned to her, and she found herself suddenly awkward and shy.

Stefan slipped on the black t-shirt he'd been wearing the night before. *We'll have to get some clothes from the apartment*, Rebecca thought.

Stefan put the breakfast tray on his bed and then grabbed Rebecca's hands . . . "Wait," he said, pulling her into the dark guest room.

The room was small and surrounded by wood paneling. The long window on the far side across from the door looked out into the large back yard and alley way. Little sun came through the windows, so the room stayed cool in the summer time and was perpetually dark. Mary had tried to brighten it up with colors of light sage green and peach, but still, it remained shadowed. Rebecca liked it. At the back of the house, it was quiet, and she would often spend time sitting in the white wicker chair by the window looking outside. But this was Stefan's room now, and she would be staying out. When he pulled her in, her stomach leaped, and she wanted to bolt out of the room while also wanting to run to Stefan. She didn't understand these feelings. He was a friend to her, but she wanted to make him feel better. She wanted his hurt to go away.

"I'm going to need you, Rebecca," Stefan said. "I need you by my side."

She nodded. Words would not come to her. She wanted to tell him never to kiss her again, but she longed to feel his lips on hers once more.

"I'm sorry about last night. I'm so full of emotion. I don't know what I'm doing. I've always had feelings for you, but I didn't want to ruin our friendship. I just . . . well . . . Can we just . . . " He looked down at his bare feet and then back up to her. "Can we just live in the moment for now and not worry about what this all means?"

Rebecca nodded again, more slowly, and realized he still held her hand.

"Okay. Let's go eat," he said, and pulled her close into a quick embrace before taking the breakfast tray out of the room and down the stairs to the kitchen.

The next few days were spent calling people and making arrangements for the funeral. Rebecca never knew that Linda had been the subject of town gossip as a teenager. She had gotten pregnant her junior year of high school, and no one ever knew who Stefan's father was, but rumors flew when a high school science teacher suddenly moved out of town during the summer before Linda had Stefan.

She had petitioned for a day care in the high school. The school relented and opened a day care where Stefan spent most of his time while Linda earned her high school diploma. She also lived above Grandma's Café where she worked part-time. Stefan became a mascot of sorts for the café and worked his way through the ranks from busboy to cook before graduating high school and entering the Navy.

Now what? he wondered one day after the funeral. *Now I'm left with half a restaurant and no family.* Linda's friend, Stacy Poole, owned the other half. They had purchased the café together after working years as waitresses. It had been a dream of theirs and had eventually come true.

Now, she was dead. Stefan couldn't believe it. The Navy had given him extended leave to deal with things, but he questioned whether his dreams mattered now.

CHAPTER 10

The day of Linda Taylor's funeral was sunny and warm. The church where the ceremony was held sat on a hill looking out over the Flagstaff valley. The windows displayed a beautiful view of the San Francisco Peaks, and Linda's coffin, surrounded by blue and white flowers, lay in front of the church windows.

Rebecca was stunned by the crowd. It seemed that Linda had become a beloved member of the community. People from all over town showed up with their black suits and white corsages, and some of the women even wore hats for the occasion.

Linda had been dressed in a light blue chiffon dress. Her hands crossed over her abdomen and held blue forget-me-nots. Her face looked peaceful; and her makeup was understated and looked natural. Wisps of her reddish auburn hair cascaded down her neck and shoulders. Rebecca stood beside Stefan, who leaned down and gave his mother one last peck on the cheek. Rebecca worked hard to hold back tears, but one leaked out. Stefan noticed and took her hand and squeezed it. She leaned against him and gave him a light tap with her shoulder. They turned to take their seats but stopped when they saw Mike walking up the aisle.

Mike had seen Stefan take Rebecca's hand and had noticed the slight tap of their shoulders. A wave of jealousy clamped his gut. Mike tried to remind himself that they were just friends. Still, that small movement had an air of intimacy that he couldn't ignore.

He had been in California but came back early when he heard about Stefan's mom and the funeral. Rebecca had talked about how close she was to Linda, so Mike wanted to be there for her. Now, he wondered if he'd made a mistake.

Standing in front of Stefan and Rebecca, he wished he hadn't come. Somehow he mustered the ability to say, "I'm so sorry for your loss."

Stefan shook his hand and said, "Thanks," and brushed past him to his seat with Rebecca's family.

Mike paid his respects and found a seat close to the back. He felt uncomfortable and unwelcomed, but he remained in his seat even after the service came to a close.

The church filed out, paying their respects to the family as they left, and Mike watched Rebecca. He had to find a way to tell her how he felt . . . and yet, he feared the worst would happen. *What if she rejects me? What if I just cause her more pain?* He thought of leaving then, but he wanted to talk to her. He needed to tell Becca everything.

After the service, Stefan stood with the Kendall family at the back of the church. He kept Rebecca close as people paid their respects. When Stefan saw Mike approach him, his fist curled and his muscles flexed. It took all his energy not to hurl his fist into Mike's face. Rebecca had told Stefan everything that had happened with Mike. *Who tells a girl "I love you" and then just leaves?*

Mike came up in the line and shook Stefan's hand. "Again, I'm so sorry for your loss," he said.

Stefan took Mike's hand and pulled Mike close. He embraced him and whispered in his ear, "She's mine now. You missed your chance."

Startled, Mike glanced at Rebecca and then turned to Stefan. "Unlike you," Mike said with a slight smile, "I don't see her as a possession." He looked at Rebecca. "I have to talk to you. I'll find you later." He left the church and sped away in his Camaro.

As the last people paid their respects, Stefan grabbed Rebecca's hand and led her to his car. "Too many people," he said as he opened the rusty car door for Rebecca. He had had the car since high school. It was a rusty, orange Toyota Corolla from the '90s. He'd spent his high school years keeping it running, and thankfully, when he got home, it still ran.

"But Stefan, you have to . . . " Her voice trailed off as he closed the car door and went around to the driver's side. She worried he'd try to find Mike. *Why had he come?*

"Don't worry," he said when he was back in his seat. "We're going to the cemetery. I just wanted to talk to you alone."

They left as friends milled about in the church parking lot. Many waved to Stefan as he left. They passed the black hearse as it sat by the church, waiting to lead the caravan to the burial site. They had dispensed with the traditional carrying of the casket and opted to have the funeral home place Linda into the hearse.

Both Rebecca and Stefan avoided looking at it.

Stefan drove slowly towards the cemetery as if delaying the inevitable. He took Rebecca's hand and looked at her. She turned her body toward him so she could read his lips as he talked and drove.

"I wanted to thank you for being here for me, Rebecca," he began. "I don't know what I'd do without you."

Rebecca smiled and nodded. "It's no problem," she said.

"I hope you weren't too upset seeing Mike." Rubbing his thumb on Rebecca's hand, he said, "I need you, Rebecca. I want you to be my girlfriend. I want us to be together. I want to help you live your dream. Let's get a band together. I know some guys. I can be your manager."

Rebecca looked at him: his red hair was blowing in the breeze coming through the open window. She saw a mixture of pain and hope in his green eyes. She didn't want to cause him more pain, so she nodded. "Okay, Stefan. Let's see where it takes us."

He smiled and held her hand up and kissed it.

They arrived at the burial site, and as Linda Taylor was lowered into her grave, Rebecca and Stefan cried.

CHAPTER 11

The day had been long and exhausting. After the burial, friends and family met at Grandma's Café where Stacy Poole had cooked up all of the menu items and more . . . she put out a spread fit for the entire town. It was Linda's day, and Stacy knew this is how she would want them to celebrate.

At first, people were solemn, but then the spirit of Linda's life took over, and people started dancing and laughing. Classic rock from the '70s and '80s played from the old juke box, and people danced on the wooden stage. Feeling the vibrations through the floor and following Stefan's lead, Rebecca danced with Stefan. He held her close throughout the evening.

When they got back to the house, Rebecca was exhausted. She gave her apologies to her folks and Stefan and then went up to her room. She had been burying her emotions all day, and now, in the privacy of her room, she could let them out. She fished out her notebook from her backpack and opened it to an empty page. Slowly, she wrote:

> *Someday my love will come.*
> *Someday he'll come through the rain.*
> *He will smile then say my name.*
> *I will know who he is*
> *I will know he is the one I've waited for.*
>
> *Someday my love will come.*
> *Someday we will shine as one.*
> *He will take me from this world.*
> *He will bring me peace.*
> *I will stay at his side . . . forever.*

She didn't love Stefan. He had been a friend, and that was all. But she couldn't stand the thought of breaking his heart right now. She'd be there for him. She'd give him what he needed for now . . . for the sake of his mom . . . for the sake of their friendship . . . for the sake of his grief . . . she'd try to get over Mike.

CHAPTER 12

Despite herself, Rebecca had a good time with Stefan. They worked together in the restaurant, and Stefan started to learn sign language. Rebecca enjoyed teaching him, and they quickly worked into a rhythm at the restaurant using sign language as they worked. She enjoyed cooking with Stefan while Stacy ran the front of the restaurant with the waitstaff.

It seemed that business had picked up since Linda's death. People wanted to support Stefan, so they came to the restaurant. They also loved seeing Stefan and Rebecca together.

Before long, it was summer, and Rebecca's best friend, Christy, was coming home from college. Rebecca couldn't wait!   It would be the three musketeers back together again: Christy, Stefan, and Rebecca.

It was the middle of May when Christy finally texted Rebecca:

I'm home!! I'm coming over!

Rebecca ran to the door and threw it open as Christy climbed the front porch steps. She wore a white peasant shirt with a knee-length jean skirt and Greek-styled high strapped sandals. The white shirt brought out Christy's dark skin and black curly hair. She smiled wide and the two hugged tightly.

"OMG!" Rebecca shouted. "You're here! You're really here! I can't believe it."

Christy came in and the two ran up to Rebecca's room to share all their gossip over the last nine months.

Christy had felt bad that she couldn't see Rebecca after the accident or after Stefan's mom had passed away. She was in college in Seattle and worked as a graphic design intern with a publishing company. She wanted to graduate before 4 years and couldn't wait to start real life. In the meantime, she would help Rebecca recover from her accident and spend a summer with her best friend as if they were still teenagers.

"What do you say?" Rebecca asked after telling her about Stefan's plan of starting a band and getting ready to play in the annual summer talent show.

"Of course!" Christy agreed and started talking about a design she could do for a flyer advertising the band. "Maybe we could get some gigs to make some extra money, too."

"We could play in the café!" Rebecca said. "I'm sure Stacy wouldn't mind, and the customers will love it! We could use the dance floor—it's like a little stage already. I'll talk to Stefan and Stacy. This will be great!"

Rebecca loved having Christy home. Everything felt like it had before the accident . . . except Tommy's absence. At least the nightmares had stopped. Rebecca had spent several mornings waking up screaming after seeing Tommy's dead stare over and over. She still struggled to ride in a car during a rain storm.

Christy saw Rebecca's smile fade. "I'm sorry," she said, taking Rebecca's hands. "It will be okay. I know you loved Tommy, but you and Stefan are together now. It's like it's meant to be."

Rebecca smiled and nodded her head, and they started exploring photos for the band flyer.

CHAPTER 13

The next day after church, Rebecca went over to Christy's house. "It just might work," Christy said after Rebecca told her about talking to Stefan. He had been excited about the idea of the band playing at Grandma's Café. He thought it would help bring in even more customers.

Christy sat in a brown leather chair facing Rebecca, who sat in a tan, canvas love seat with her legs folded beneath her.

"It's hard to tell," Christy continued. "They might not believe you're deaf."

"You're probably right, but I want to do it. Besides, does it matter?"

"I guess it doesn't. But won't you have . . . problems? You know what I mean."

"Don't worry. I've been practicing with my tuner app! I'm getting pretty good at telling the difference between notes and how they feel in my throat. There's also lots of equipment to help me."

"Okay. I believe in you," Christy said as she hugged Rebecca. "I'll gather up the guys for auditions Wednesday."

♫♪♫♪

"Absolutely not," Mrs. Kendall yelled after Rebecca had told her the plans. "I don't want my little girl singing in a band."

"Why not? Because I'm DEAF?"

"Come on, Mary," Mr. Kendall begged over breakfast the next day. "It's her dream. At least let her try."

With her hands on her hips, she gave in—sort of. "Let me meet the boys who are going to play for you."

Rebecca sighed. Since the accident, Rebecca's mom had become increasingly overprotective. Rebecca tried to understand and comply with their new rules.

"Well, we don't exactly know yet. We have to audition them. They're all coming over Wednesday, and we're going to use the garage for auditions.

"Without my permission!?"

Rebecca looked blankly at her mother . . . surprised by what seemed to be anger on her mother's face.

"I'm sorry, Mom," she signed. "I didn't think about asking."

Mrs. Kendall sighed. "I'll let it pass. But ask me next time."

Rebecca nodded. "Thanks."

Wednesday finally arrived, and shortly after lunch, a group of people showed up on the doorstep. Stefan let them in and introduced them to Mr. and Mrs. Kendall.

"This is Richard Mitchell; he plays the drums." One side of his mouth rose in a smile as he looked down at Mrs. Kendall.

"How do you do?" he asked as he shook Mrs. Kendall's hand.

"Fine, thank you," she answered.

With a stern lecture, Mrs. Kendall agreed to allow her daughter to sing with the group. As a surprise, Mr. Kendall had spoken with the band director Mr. Walker at the college. He was allowing them to use the band room on campus, but they were instructed to leave the room better than they had found it. Rebecca and the crew nodded. Summer classes hadn't started yet, so they could meet anytime. "After summer school starts, you will have to find another space." Mr. Walker told them.

Stefan had to leave for work at the restaurant, but everyone else drove to the college and settled into the band room for auditions.

Rebecca called the members into the room one-by-one, and Christy asked them questions. Each played a part of a song they had prepared.

The auditions went pretty well. Rebecca watched the tuner to see if they played in tune, but she relied on Christy's judgment on the band members' abilities. They talked about who to pick for the band.

"We'll announce the band tomorrow," Rebecca said.

"So, who are the band members?" Christy asked.

"Well, for piano, there's Jimmy Carton or Burton Smith. For drums, Robert Michaels or Richard Mitchell."

"How about Burton for piano and Richard for drums. Who's our manager?"

"You. For guitar, there's . . . "

"Hold on! I'm the manager?"

"Yep." Rebecca kept looking at the papers on the table. "Who should I let play bass guitar?" she asked and then looked up at Christy.

"I can't believe it!" Christy was surprised, thinking Stefan would be manager.

"Look. You'll share it with Stefan, okay?"

"Oh, okay. That sounds good. Who do we have for bass guitar?"

"There's Eric Dinney or Daniel Bailey."

"They're both good."

"Yeah. Well, what we could do is have one on bass and the other on acoustic."

"Okay. Great."

"Both of them can play both parts."

"Put Danny on bass."

"Sounds like a plan."

"Now what do we need?"

"I'm not sure. Backup singers?"

"So, that's covered."

"We need someone who will help with equipment."

"Uh, Mark Linley or Ted Birk?"

"Mark."

"Okay. We have it: Burton on piano, Richard on drums, Danny on bass guitar, Eric on acoustic, and Mark on equipment."

"And me for manager," Christy reminded her.

"And backup singer along with everyone else. Lead singer: me."

"And Stefan?" Christy asked.

"He'll help as manager when you're not singing."

"He can help with equipment, too."

Rebecca looked down at the papers and shrugged.

"What's up, girl?" Christy asked. "Don't you want Stefan to be involved?"

"Of course I do . . . it's just that . . . well, I don't know where it's going . . . so it's better that he's not too involved. You know what I mean?"

Christy shrugged. "Okay. As long as you know what you're doing. I better get you home. My mom has some family shindig planned for my homecoming, and I can't be late."

"Thanks, Christy."

♪♪♪

The next day, Rebecca texted the new band members and asked them to meet at the college band room that afternoon.

"We have a melody for this song," Christy started.

"What song is it?" Burton interrupted Christy.

"A song Rebecca wrote."

"Cool."

"We also have the harmony down, but it needs some background music, mostly bass and drums."

"I can help," Richard butted in. "I'm good with that kind of stuff."

"Okay, you'll be working with Rebecca."

"Cool."

"I'll help with bass," Danny said as he stepped forward.

"Ok, you're working with me," Christy said while pointing to Danny.

The rest of the band members left. Rebecca and Richard went to work on the drums. Christy and Danny worked on the bass guitar.

They worked most of the afternoon and evening trying to get the parts solidified for the song. Things began to take shape when Mr. Walker, came in. "Aren't you kids going home?" he asked as he scratched his balding head.

"Sure," Christy answered.

There was a laugh from the corner where Rebecca and Richard were working.

Richard was telling a story about when he got a pant leg torn off by a poodle. He let out a rumble of laughter as Rebecca looked up at Mr. Walker.

"Violence isn't always funny," Mr. Walker said as Richard got ahold of himself.

"Sorry, Mr. Walker. Just a little joke."

"I understand." And he smiled. "How's the rhythm section coming?" Rebecca looked at Richard and let out a little snicker.

"What's so funny?" Mr. Walker asked, wanting in on the joke.

Richard tried to keep from laughing as he answered the questions. "We're not doing very well."

"And why not?"

"Rhythm's hard to come by," Rebecca answered. "It's hard to feel the vibrations with the bass guitar playing at the same time. I also think I need to tweak the lyrics some. We have some patterns, but we can't fit them together."

"All you need is one basic pattern, and you've got it made."

"Yeah, and all we need is that one basic pattern," Richard answered as he got up off the floor.

"You kids better get home before the janitors come," Mr. Walker continued as he walked out of the band room onto the stage. "Tryouts for the talent show are in one week."

"One week?!" they shouted in unison. The talent show wasn't until July, so it didn't make sense to try out so early.

"Why so early?" Christy asked.

"They want time to advertise the bands. We want a huge audience. It's a big deal, you know. If you win this, you could go far in your musical career. The grand prize is a recording deal on top of the prize money."

The band looked at each other one-by-one trying to keep their excitement from overflowing too much.

"Well, we better figure out some songs to play by next week," Rebecca said. "My song won't be ready by then."

"That's all right." Mr. Walker answered. "It doesn't have to be an original song. It will help for the final round—if you make it that far—but otherwise, the songs can be covers."

They all nodded, each devising a plan for their success.

"I'd better get home," Richard said, looking at his phone. "Would you like a ride home, Rebecca? I have my dad's car."

"Sure!" Rebecca jumped up and followed Richard out with Christy and Danny behind her.

"Hey, maybe this Friday we can double date," Danny suggested.

Richard stopped, and Rebecca ran into him.

"Why did we stop?" she asked, not being able to read their lips.

Richard stepped aside and put his hand on her back. "Danny suggested something," Richard answered, looking down at her.

Danny glanced over at Christy as she stood wide-eyed and smiling strangely. Danny was short and almost reached the top of Christy's head.

"Anything wrong?" Danny asked.

"No," Christy answered. "You just suggest strange things."

"Would somebody please tell me what's going on?" Rebecca shouted desperately.

"Sorry," Richard apologized. "Danny suggested that we double date Friday."

"Sounds like fun," Rebecca answered as she smiled at everyone. Christy gave her a desperate look. "Why not? We could grab a car and go to the drive-in, or hey, I know, we could go to that outside country concert."

"Real funny," Danny said, recognizing her joke.

Rebecca laughed and shrugged. She knew most of them didn't like country music, and watching a movie wasn't easy for her without subtitles, which didn't always exist in a movie theater, especially at a drive-in, an old relic from the '70s.

"Now wait a minute . . . " Christy protested.

"No, I mean it." Danny said. "It would be fun. You and me, Richard and Rebecca."

Rebecca turned to face him. "But . . . " she tried to interrupt. She didn't think they were serious. Besides, she technically had a boyfriend.

Richard turned around and walked toward his father's gray Camry parked right behind the band room in the loading zone.

"What do you say?" Danny asked Richard as he reached his car.

"If you drive, it's okay with me," he answered as he opened the passenger door for Rebecca. They climbed in and watched Christy toss her hands up in the air in defeat and follow Danny reluctantly to his car.

"I guess I'll give in," Christy said as she began to laugh. Richard got in and started the car.

"What happened to your car?" Rebecca asked.

"Oh. It's on the fritz. Good ol' Chevy truck finally took its last drive, I'm afraid." He backed the car up and drove out of the parking lot on his way to Rebecca's house.

Richard felt the need to explain to Rebecca. "I hope you didn't think that I didn't want to double date on Friday. I just couldn't believe Danny said that. Just yesterday he had said Christy was too tall for him. I just joined in for Christy's sake."

They stopped in front of Rebecca's house. She began to open the door, but Richard stopped her with a touch.

"In fact, let's you and I go out alone sometime—just the two of us."

"I can't do that. I can't double date with you either. You can go with Christy and Danny, but take whoever you want." She opened the door and Richard stopped her from getting out.

"Rebecca, please. I want to do something with you."

"I'm sorry, but I'm busy. I thought you were joking. I also don't think I should date band members. I'll see you tomorrow after work for practice." She got out and closed the door and rushed up the sidewalk to her front door.

"Well, it's about time," Stefan said with a smile as Rebecca entered the living room. He had still been living with them since the funeral. He couldn't yet face his mother's apartment above the café.

Stefan met her halfway and gave her a quick kiss on the lips.

"Band practice. What's for dinner?" Rebecca asked as she sat on the couch next to Stefan.

"Who knows. Your mom and dad are still at the store. Who gave you a lift home?"

"Richard. He's part of the band."

"What's wrong? You seem sad."

Rebecca shook her head. "I'm okay." She did feel sad. Although she was enjoying the band and working at the restaurant, she couldn't help but feel like something was missing. And she knew that something was Mike. She had loved Tommy, but she loved Mike more. Although they weren't together, they shared a kind of intimacy that she hadn't known possible. Having him gone was like having a part of her ripped from her existence.

She also felt guilty for loving Mike, dating Stefan, and not telling Richard about Stefan. She felt stuck and didn't know what to do.

14

The days passed slowly, and Rebecca painted on a smile every morning before she left her room. The band progressed and so did Rebecca's singing. She quit working on writing new poems and songs and focused on the old, throwing out lines here and there.

For the talent show auditions, the band decided to play a cover of an old Tom Petty song—one that didn't require a lot of singing. Although Rebecca had been practicing with the app, she wasn't quite confident that her singing was on point. She had to trust the technology and trust that the pitch in her head was the one she produced for the audience. It was nerve-wracking, but with a mix of rap and singing and lots of drum and guitar solos, they made it through the auditions. The band was up for the talent show.

Rebecca's band was on the list as one of three main attractions. The talent show poster listed the name of the band in gold letters: The Dream Catchers.

"How about that? We're a main attraction!" Christy rejoiced.

"The Dream Catchers? What kind of name is that?" Burton Smith asked.

"That sounds stupid," Eric Benny replied.

"It was the first thing that came to mind. They kinda put me on the spot." Christy mimicked the talent show crew. "'What's the name of the band? Come on. You can't be famous without a name?' So what could I say? We hadn't even talked about it!"

"Yeah, but still . . . " Eric teased.

"Come on, Rebecca," Richard begged. "You can't be busy every night."

"You can be with my schedule," she replied. Everyone was talking at once, and it was hard for Mark Linley, the equipment manager, to get their attention. Mark had meant to be an assistant to Stefan, but since Stefan worked so much at the restaurant, Mark found himself in charge of the equipment. That made Christy backup singer and general manager.

"May I have your attention?" he shouted desperately as everyone roared on. Mark was a big guy, but it was hard for him to speak out because he was shy. Although he looked intimidating, everyone knew he was a pushover. He was an expert, though, when it came to computers and recording equipment.

Finally, the group began to settle down, and Mark could speak without yelling. "Now we pulled off the auditions with a popular song, which Rebecca sang very well." There was a short applause and Mark continued. "Now, we have to get serious and rehearse this song Rebecca wrote for the talent show." There was another short applause. He continued after clearing his throat. "There are two rounds before the final. We'll play popular songs for the first two rounds. I have that list. Then we'll play Rebecca's song for the final round. Might be an encore as a tie breaker, too, by Mr. Walker's request, so we'll need to have something planned for that. That should cover it. Let's get to work."

They worked every day late into the night after Rebecca finished her shift at the restaurant. Finally, it began to take shape. Rebecca's heart began to mend, and she rarely had time to think about Mike.

Richard kept asking for dates. She finally gave in despite her feelings of guilt. Although she was technically dating Stefan, he still didn't feel like her boyfriend, especially since he worked so much. Rebecca felt like she was living two lives: her life at the restaurant with Stefan, and her life with the band. They rarely met.

It was a cloudless night and kind of cool. It was the first part of June when the days were getting long and turning warmer. It was just an innocent coffee and a drive around town.

"I don't know much about you," Richard told Rebecca as they sat in the coffee shop off Main Street.

"There's not much to know," Rebecca answered as she watched the people in the café disappear. She made sure they were far from Grandma's Café ... but she was still nervous about running into Stefan.

Although she insisted they weren't on a date, she still worried about explaining it to Stefan.

"Why have you been ignoring me the last month?"

"Personal reasons."

"Can you give me a hint?"

Rebecca finished her coffee and looked out the window. The sun was somewhere beyond the mountains, and Rebecca was sinking with it. *I don't know if I can last the evening*, she thought. *I need to be home at 10 so I can get up for work, and it's only 8:30.* She turned toward Richard who had finished his coffee and was looking at Rebecca.

"See? You're still doing it," he said.

"Doing what?" Rebecca asked innocently.

"Ignoring me."

"Oh, I'm sorry." The waiter brought the check. They got up and paid it.

"So, where to?" Rebecca asked as they exited the café. "You do realize you can't talk to me unless we're in the light?"

Richard nodded and opened the door for Rebecca. He went to the driver's side and climbed in. He turned on the light inside of the car and said one thing. "What I have planned doesn't call for much talking." He switched off the light, and Rebecca began to worry.

Richard started the car, and they left the café. Rebecca stared out the window.

They passed a little convenience store when Rebecca glanced at a blue Camaro parked under a light. *Mike's back*, she thought. They pulled up to the little store. Richard said something as he got out of the car. Rebecca stared at the car in disbelief. The license plate number read MNC267. *That's Mike's car,* she thought. *Mike is probably inside.*

"Rebecca, come on." Richard opened the door and persuaded Rebecca out of the car. "There's someone inside who wants to see you." Richard had come out of the store and pulled Rebecca in before she could resist.

Rebecca entered the door with her head down. She looked up and saw Mike smiling.

"Hi," he said.

Rebecca froze. For so long she had struggled to keep him out of her mind, and now here he was standing in front of her in a little store where she couldn't run up and hug him or hit him or whatever else she wanted to do.

"Hi," she struggled to say.

"Long time no see."

"Yeah, I know. I heard you were out of town."

Mike nodded. "I was in California taking care of some family business."

"How's your family?" Rebecca asked.

"Fine. Would you like to go for a drive?"

"I can't. I'm with Richard." She shuffled her feet.

"Oh? Where's Stefan?"

Rebecca blushed and turned to Richard, who saved her from admitting guilt. "Would you like to drive around a bit and catch up?" he asked Mike.

"No, I don't want to interfere. Besides I have to get home. My house is . . . " His words trailed off, and he shrugged his shoulders. He couldn't give away the surprise just yet.

"Okay, find yourself a girl, and maybe we can double date just for old times' sake."

"Yeah, maybe. Better go. Nice seeing you again. Really, Becca." He lingered a few seconds longer, looking Rebecca in the eyes, and then he walked toward the door.

Rebecca hollered after him. "Stop by the house sometime. I'm sure my mom would like to see you." Rebecca couldn't believe what she had just said. Maybe she wanted him to get beaten up by Stefan . . . maybe it was just habit.

"Maybe I will," he said as he smiled. He disappeared behind the door and drove away as Rebecca and Richard came out.

I hurt her, Mike thought as he remembered the look in her eyes. It was an empty look, like she had lost someone dear to her. *The spark in her eyes is missing.* Mike drove on and intended to get the spark lit again. *I'm tired of hurting her.*

CHAPTER 15

The weekend passed with Rebecca looking out for Mike. She didn't tell Stefan about seeing Mike, afraid he would be looking for him, too. Rebecca was disappointed by the time Monday came.

"He didn't say he would come by this weekend," Christy reassured Rebecca as they walked to rehearsal.

"Yeah, I know, but if he was happy to see me, he would've come by Saturday," Rebecca complained.

"Maybe that's why he didn't come so soon."

"What do you mean?"

"Never mind. I'll tell you later. We need to focus on rehearsal." Rebecca sat down in her seat. She was glad for the distraction.

After rehearsal, Rebecca went straight home while the other band members went out for drinks. She refused rides because she preferred to walk home. As

Rebecca walked home, she looked for Mike's car, but she didn't see it.

"Hi," her mother greeted as she entered the kitchen. "How was rehearsal?"

"Okay for a Monday," Rebecca answered, pouring milk into a glass. "I'll be in the study writing." Rebecca went into the study and closed the door behind her. She didn't have a lot of writing to do, and she didn't feel like doing any because she wanted to be alone. Stefan was at the restaurant where he had been spending most of his time. So, she enjoyed the time alone and read her book while sitting in the study. The time passed, and Rebecca started downstairs for a late snack. Her mother met her in the hallway.

"Christy is downstairs dying to talk to you. She said you didn't respond to her texts," she said.

"Oh. Yeah. My phone and watch are charging in my room. Thanks, Mom," Rebecca answered. She followed her mother down the stairs and saw Christy talking to Stefan in the living room. She hadn't realized Stefan was back from the restaurant.

"Hi," Rebecca welcomed.

"Hey. I've got to talk to you," Christy answered.

"Let's sit outside," Rebecca said, turning to Stefan. "Would you mind making some popcorn?"

Stefan nodded. The two girls went on the porch and sat down on the steps.

"What is it?" Rebecca asked faintly.

"I'm worried," Christy answered.

It was cool, and the sun was beginning to sink behind the mountains. It was a wonderful June evening.

"About what?"

"You."

"Tell me why, Christy. You know you shouldn't be."

"There's a rumor going around Facebook, and it's been careful to leave you out."

"What rumor?"

"It's about Mike," Christy paused and Rebecca waited patiently.

"There's some story about him getting into some trouble with some girl."

"What?"

"I don't want to hurt you. Mike is transferring to UCLA because he has a girlfriend in Los Angeles. He's been lying to you."

"What?" Rebecca stood up.

"They're engaged. He's here to sell his house and move there to get married." Rebecca stiffened trying not to care. She didn't even know he owned a house. She thought he lived on campus. The half-spoken sentence about Mike's house made sense now. He would be putting it on the market.

She took a deep breath and stood up straighter. "Don't worry about it," she said. "I'm over him."

"I don't think you are. I think that seeing him has reminded you how much you still want to be with him. Think about it. You've been waiting for him to stop by. He's not going to."

Rebecca nodded. "Thanks, Christy. I'm glad you told me.

"Now get that look off your face. Stefan's coming."

Stefan came out and looked at Rebecca's worried face. "The popcorn is ready, and I thought we'd watch a movie with subtitles." He winked.

"Thanks, Stefan. Do you want to watch a movie with us, Christy?"

"No. I need to get up early tomorrow. But I'll see you at rehearsal."

Rebecca nodded, and they hugged good-bye. "See you tomorrow."

Now what? Rebecca thought as she settled in with Stefan and an action movie. She had no idea what movie they watched . . . her mind raced the entire time about Mike.

The week passed, and it was Friday night before Rebecca allowed herself to think about Mike again. She had kept busy on purpose. Now, she was sitting in the living room waiting for her parents to return from their outing. Once again, she was alone while Stefan was working at the restaurant. Rebecca let her mind wander, and she began to think of Mike. She shook the thought of him out of her mind and looked for something to do. A red light began to blink on and off over the living room doorway. Her smartwatch buzzed. "Doorbell." She went to answer the door.

"Mike!" Rebecca was startled. "Come on in." She held open the door. Mike came in and waited until Rebecca shut the door before he spoke.

"I've missed you a lot, Becca." She looked deeply into his eyes, forgetting her manners. She wanted to jump into his arms and forget everything. "I need to talk to you," Mike signed.

"I need to talk to you, too." Rebecca remembered her conversation with Christy just a few days ago. She held back her eagerness for answers.

She welcomed him in, and they sat on the couch.

"I'm sorry I haven't been in touch with you since Linda's funeral," he began. "I have been busy with some family business." Rebecca was quiet, waiting for Mike to continue, but he didn't.

What would he say now? she thought. He would tell me about his girlfriend. "I understand," Rebecca said out loud. "Is that all?"

"Should there be more?"

"No." It wasn't the right moment to let Mike know what was on her mind, but how was she to tell him?

"What are you thinking?" Mike waited patiently as Rebecca went through her thoughts.

Finally, she spoke. "I'm not sure if now is the right moment."

"Look," Mike said as he put his hand on her knee. By now, they were sitting pretty close to each other in the middle of the couch. "You can tell me whatever is on your mind."

Rebecca struggled to say something, but she couldn't. *I'll tell him*, she thought, *but later.*

Mike interrupted her thoughts. "There's someone coming in the door."

"I'll get it." She got up and went to the door, relieved they were interrupted.

Stefan hurried in, soaking wet from the early summer downpour. He rushed to Rebecca and picked her up. "It's so good to see you. I've had a rough day!"

"Stefan, you're getting me wet!" she said as she laughed.

He kissed her as he slowly set her back down. "It's cold out there," he said. "Come warm me up." He took her hand and started to lead her upstairs. She resisted, and Mike interrupted them with a hello.

Stefan dropped Rebecca's hand and started for Mike.

"Stefan!" Rebecca grabbed Stefan's arm to stop him from getting closer to Mike. She feared he'd hit him.

"Great time for you to show up," Stefan said, his body tense.

"Decided to come back. California isn't my kind of place," Mike answered.

"You're playing dangerously," Stefan said.

"You think so, huh?" Mike said, getting defensive.

"Should've stayed in California with the party girls."

"Why? I've got all I need right here." He smiled at Rebecca, who noticed the anger in Stefan's eyes.

"I think you better go, Mike." Stefan started to show him to the door.

"I'm not going anywhere. I came to get what's mine," he said, walking to Rebecca.

Rebecca didn't know what to do. She was with Stefan, but she loved Mike. She wanted to grab his hand and run out the door, but instead, she just stood there. That's when Stefan punched Mike.

Mike fell—his limbs sprawled out on the floor and his lip bleeding.

"You broke a promise!" Stefan yelled. "It'll take a while for the damage you've done to mend."

Rebecca ran to Mike and bent down to his side as he sat up and brushed the blood from his lip. She couldn't help herself. She put herself in between Stefan and Mike, hoping to calm the situation. "Just stop, Stefan!" she yelled.

"Look. I deserved that," Mike said, standing up. "But I've come here to make things right."

"You can't make them right," Stefan said, "except by leaving."

"No!" Rebecca yelled, amazed by the overflow of emotion she felt. The boys flinched as if her voice had struck them both. They stopped posturing and looked at Rebecca.

"Who's it going to be, Rebecca? Me or him?" Stefan asked with his arms folded over his chest.

"I'm sorry," Mike signed.

Rebecca looked at Stefan and then at Mike. A tear rolled down her face. She wiped at it furiously as many began pouring out. "I don't know," she cried. "Don't make me choose, Stefan. I can't!" Rebecca ran up the stairs.

Mike looked at Stefan. "Look. I came to win her back, and that's exactly what I'm going to do. I'll be back." Mike wiped the blood off his lip and then left.

Stefan ran up to Rebecca's room, but she had locked her door. He could hear her sobbing on the other side. He left her alone and went to his room and closed the door. He worried he'd lost her for good.

CHAPTER 16

The next morning Rebecca stayed in bed for a long time before she was ready to face another day. She hoped Stefan would understand why she wouldn't be at the restaurant that day. When she got out of bed, the sun was high and the day was half over. She got dressed after a shower and went downstairs.

"Good morning," her father greeted.

"'Morning," Rebecca replied

"Would you like some breakfast?" her mother asked. She was washing dishes, and Mr. Kendall was fixing the door to the garage. Apparently, he was taking a coffee break. He was sitting on the floor sipping a cup of coffee.

"More like lunch," her father commented.

"I'd like some orange juice, Mom," Rebecca answered heading for the refrigerator.

Mrs. Kendall got Rebecca a glass, and Rebecca filled it with orange juice. "Why didn't you tell me Mike was back in town?" Mrs. Kendall asked. Rebecca didn't say anything. She just looked at her mother quizzically. "He came by this morning looking for you. He and Stefan went for a drive."

"He came by last night, too." Rebecca said.

"Oh, yeah?" Mr. Kendall got interested as he rinsed his coffee cup.

"We were talking when Stefan came in from work."

"Did you invite him over?" Mrs. Kendall asked as she sat down at the table.

"He just showed up. Did you have fun on your date last night?" Rebecca tried to change the subject.

"Yes, we did." Mrs. Kendall answered. "Are you okay, Rebecca? I'm worried about you."

Rebecca looked at her mom and decided to tell her about her problems. "I'm all right. I'm just confused is all. Stefan wants us to be together, but I'm in love with Mike. But Mike is . . . I don't know . . . acting so strangely, and then there's this rumor going on about him that he's engaged. And . . . every time we try to talk, we get interrupted. I don't know what's going on."

It all came flooding out as if a water pipe had broken. She hoped her mom wouldn't judge her too harshly. "You said Mike and Stefan went for a drive?"

Mrs. Kendall nodded.

Rebecca frowned and shook her head. "Well, Stefan punched Mike yesterday. I hope they're not killing each other now."

Just then, Mrs. Kendall heard the front door open. "I think they're back. We'll find out." Rebecca walked around the kitchen wall, through the dining room, and into the living room. Mike and Stefan seemed to be laughing. Rebecca looked confused.

"What? Now you're best friends?" she asked.

Stefan stepped toward Rebecca and touched her arm. "Look, Rebecca. I'm sorry about last night. We'll work it out. I just want you to be happy. Why don't you take some time to figure out what you want. In the meantime, I'm going to move back home. I think it's been long enough, and I need to face my mom's stuff sometime."

Numb with confusion, Rebecca stared at Stefan. Rebecca felt her mom behind her, and Mary stepped forward to greet Mike. "Come in," she said and signaled for him to sit down.

"That's okay," Mike said. "I was hoping Becca and I could take a walk."

"Sure," Rebecca said. "Let me get my jacket and shoes. I'll be down in a minute."

Mike nodded, and Stefan slapped Mike on the back. "Let's take a look at your car and see if we can fix it." Mike nodded in agreement.

"Something's wrong with your car?" Rebecca asked with curiosity.

"Squeaky door is all," Mike replied.

Rebecca smiled as the two boys went out the door. Mrs. Kendall followed Rebecca upstairs to talk.

"What is it about boys?" Rebecca asked. "They can be fighting one minute and best friends the next."

Mary laughed. "That's true. They're not like women who hold grudges. But it looks like this might work out.

It seems that Stefan knows how you feel. Open up to Mike. It's not good to hold it all in."

Rebecca nodded, considering her advice.

♫♫♫

Stefan got the tools out of the garage as Mike unlocked his car and plugged his phone into the stereo to play some tunes. When Stefan returned, Mike began to talk about what was on his mind.

"Thanks for understanding, Stefan," Mike said. "I'm glad we could talk this out."

"Yep." Stefan laid out the tools they would need. Mike opened and closed the door on the passenger's side. It made a slight squeaking noise. Stefan shook his head. "I think it's just a loose bolt." He began to make adjustments on the door after he climbed into the car. "About last night . . . I'm sorry I hit you. Could you hand me that screwdriver?" Mike looked on the sidewalk and found the tool and handed it to Stefan.

"It wasn't really my fault her heart was broken. I had to go to California." Mike began to get jittery. He went to the driver's side and grabbed an e-cigarette off the dashboard. He puffed on the tube and blew out a cloud of vapor. Stefan looked at him, surprised.

"I didn't know you vaped." Stefan began to work on the door once more.

"I just started again. I used to smoke when I was younger. I gave it up for girls."

"Now you're starting again? For what reason?"

"Girls. One in particular. They're annoying sometimes."

Stefan nodded. "So, look, after last night, I did some thinking, and I realized that Rebecca and I are not meant to be together. She's more of a friend to me than a girlfriend. We tried, but the chemistry really isn't there. I don't think we could ever make it work. I think I was just drawn to her out of grief for my mom. Besides, I have plans that don't involve settling down."

"I get it." Mike said and took a drag from his e-cigarette. "I told you my plans, and I appreciate your support. Find anything wrong with the door?"

"The screw just needed a little tightening. Let's try it now." They both got out of the car. Stefan swung the door back and forth. It made no sound. Then he closed it all the way and opened it again as far as it would go. "It's fixed."

"Great." Mike put his e-cigarette back in the car and helped Stefan pick up the tools.

"Listen," Stefan said as they headed for the garage. "I don't have anything against you personally. In fact, I think you're a nice guy, but I don't want to see Rebecca get hurt. Do you understand?"

"Yeah, I do. I don't want to hurt her, but sometimes . . . " Stefan wouldn't let him finish.

"I won't accept any 'buts.' Sometimes you have to admit to yourself that you hurt her, and she'll never be the same. All I'm asking is that you admit it to me, too, but only when you've admitted it to yourself." Mike was silent as they put the tools away.

Finally, Mike spoke while he turned off his phone. "I have already admitted it to myself and pretty soon Rebecca will know my plans just like you know."

"That's good. You're on the right track. Just hope she's forgiven you."

Rebecca came out of the house just as they were heading for the door.

"I'm ready," she said to Mike. She turned to Stefan and gave him a kiss on the cheek. "Thank you," she said.

"See you later!" Stefan called after them as the couple headed for the car.

Mike opened the door for Rebecca and praised Stefan for the good work. "See, it doesn't squeak." he said.

"I never knew it did," Rebecca replied with a laugh.

Mike got in and started the engine. "Any place in particular?" he asked.

"Nope, just take me beyond the horizon of the hills."

"Where's that?"

"Above and beyond."

"You're not making sense."

"Oh, just never mind. Just a song I'm working on. Drive, would you?"

"All right, my princess." Mike laughed.

They drove around town and stopped to talk to some people Mike knew. "Hey, Mike! How's life goin' for you?" one guy asked as Rebecca and Mike got out of the car.

"Oh, pretty well," Mike answered.

"It looks like it with a pretty girl on one side and a nice lookin' car under you." He began circling the car, touching it with his round fingers and looking inside. "Nice."

"Well, Mike. Long time no see." A girl braiding her long, blonde hair walked out of the little store.

"Hi, Melissa." Mike walked up to her and gave her a little hug. "What have you been doing with yourself?"

"Oh, nothin'. Just hangin' around ol' Berny there." She nodded her head to the guy who was now climbing into Mike's car. "I see you got yourself a new girl." She nodded toward Rebecca who was standing behind Mike.

"Oh yeah. Melissa this is Becca." He turned around and put his arm around Rebecca, bringing her closer to him. "She's not really a new girl. I met her last year."

Rebecca realized it had almost been a year since the accident with Tommy. How things had changed!

"Hey, Mike, come take me for a spin," Berny yelled from the car.

"Hold on," he turned toward Melissa. "Why don't you two get acquainted, and I'll show Berny what my car has to offer. Be back soon." He left, and Melissa took Rebecca into the store.

"This is my store and my home," Melissa said.

It was a cute store with a coffee bar. They went behind the bar and entered a small room with a bed and a dresser.

"So you still stick with Mike after all the rumors that have been going around?" She got two coffees and gave one to Rebecca. "Or, do you know about the rumors?"

"Yeah, I do, but Mike doesn't know I know. I'll talk to him about them and see what happens," Rebecca answered. They sat down on the couch and drank their coffee.

"I know Mike. If he likes you, he'll completely shut you off, and he won't talk to you for a while. That's only if you know the truth. If it's a lie, he'll deny it."

"So, he's a liar?" Rebecca asked.

"Not really," Melissa explained. She talked about how they met and explained that Mike had gotten in trouble in California a few years ago.

"He was tutoring this young girl—about 16, I'd say, and the girl made a move on Mike. He didn't really reciprocate, but the mother saw them kissing. Next thing you know, she's claiming statutory rape and sexual harassment. It was awful. He had to promise to marry the girl to get the family to leave him alone. He came here to get away from it for a while . . . plus, the internship and scholarship at NAU helped. Then I guess he met you. How did you two meet?"

Rebecca told her the story about Tommy, the accident, and how Mike had been helping her manage living life in a hearing world.

"He's a good guy," Melissa said. "He just lets his heart dictate things rather than his head."

Rebecca could see that, and she knew she was the same way. She wondered if they could have a future together with such a mix.

After Mike and Berny came back, Mike took Rebecca and they got into his car. "Come back soon," Melissa called as Mike drove away.

"So, do you like Melissa?" Mike asked.

"Yeah," Becca answered.

"Something wrong? You haven't said much for a while."

"Just thinking." Rebecca glanced out the window at the little houses and stores. "I haven't been in this part of town for a long time," Rebecca said as she turned toward Mike.

"Yeah, me either. I have something to show you."

They drove out of town quite a ways and then stopped in front of a little yellow and white farm house. Rebecca smiled when she saw it.

The L-shaped house was small with a wooden screen door and a small porch. A porch swing sat just to the left of the front door. Parts of the house had fresh paint, and the windows looked new with fresh white trim. The grounds surrounding the house were buried in weeds, but a small corral sat to the left of the house and trees surrounded the property, providing plenty of shade.

"Where are we?" Rebecca asked.

"My aunt lived here until she died a few years ago. I used to visit almost every summer when I was little. She left it to me in her will. I haven't been using it—living on campus seemed easier. I thought about selling it, but I've decided not to.

"I like it," Rebecca said as she walked across the tall grass to the porch.

The house needed some TLC, but she could see that Mike had painted part of it, and some of the steps were new.

"Can we go in?" Rebecca asked.

Mike smiled and nodded. "Before we do, there's something I want to say." He took Rebecca's hands and held them. "Becca, if something is on your mind, don't be afraid to talk to me about it."

She looked at their joined hands and then up at Mike. "It's something Melissa said."

"Yeah?" Mike waited patiently as Rebecca gathered up her thoughts.

"She said that if I asked you a question or said something about you that was true, you would shut yourself off completely, but if it wasn't true, you would deny it."

Mike was quiet at first. "What made her say that?" he finally asked.

Rebecca thought of keeping quiet, but she remembered her mother's advice and told him the whole conversation. Mike was quiet as he listened.

"Let's finish this conversation inside," he said as they entered the house.

The wooden floors creaked as they walked through the front hallway into the living room. The furniture looked dated and worn, but cozy. She could see a woman's touch in the room: a crocheted doily on the side table next to a blue-striped chair, paintings of birds and garden scenes, and tied rag rugs under the coffee table and dotted across the wooden floors.

"Let me give you a tour," he said.

Mike led Rebecca through the living room and into the kitchen. She could imagine a woman fixing Thanksgiving dinner in the country kitchen, unloading dishes from the light blue cabinets, and setting the loose-leaf table just off to the side in the dining room.

From the kitchen, a door opened onto a covered porch.

"It's beautiful, Mike," Rebecca said.

Mike smiled and motioned for her to have a seat on the cushioned white wicker couch.

After enjoying the view, Mike and Rebecca sat down in the living room. "Would you like something to drink?" Mike asked.

"Sure. I'd take a soda if you have one," Rebecca answered.

"Yep, I'll be right back." Mike went to get a soda in the kitchen while Rebecca enjoyed the view of the Coconino Forest in full summer bloom: yellow and purple flowers spotted the valley.

Mike came back with two sodas and set them on the coffee table. He sat down on the couch next to Rebecca.

"Well, how do you like my house?"

"I like it! It's cozy." Rebecca said taking a sip of soda. She liked the feel of the cold carbonation flowing down her throat, and she smiled at the bottle.

Mike sipped his soda and smiled. "Now tell me about the rumors," Mike said, getting serious.

Oh no, Rebecca thought. "Well," she began out loud. "I guess it's all over Facebook." She took another sip of her soda.

"Tell me about it, please, Rebecca." Mike was being patient as he looked at her.

"I was told that you had a girlfriend in Los Angeles." Rebecca held her breath. *Deny it*, she thought. *Please, Mike. If you love me, you'll deny it.*

The surprise left his eyes. "I can't deny it, but it's not true. It's complicated, but yeah, there used to be a girl in Los Angeles."

"Does she mean anything to you?"

"You mean more to me than anyone ever will."
Rebecca smiled and moved closer to Mike. He put
his arm around her and kissed her. His lips were soft;
it was hard to stop. Rebecca wanted the kiss to go on
all night, but she pulled away.

"That wasn't all, Mike," she continued.

He looked at her and smiled. "Okay, tell me the
rest."

"This probably isn't true either, but . . . " she paused.
"I was also told that you were engaged and that you
were accused of sexual harassment from the girl's
mother." Mike frowned. He lifted his arm and moved
to the edge of the couch. He looked away and then
turned back to Rebecca. Without a word, he got up
and went into the kitchen.

Oh no, Rebecca thought. *Now what will I do? He's
upset. It's true.* A tear rolled down her cheek, and she
wiped it away. She struggled to hold back others as
Mike walked in with a bag of potato chips. He set the
bag on the table and sat back down beside Rebecca.

"I suppose I better start explaining." He took a
potato chip out of the bag and offered one to Rebecca,
who refused. "You see, this girl in Los Angeles had
been a client—my first client. She was young—like 16.
I knew she had a crush on me, and I didn't really know
how to handle it. I ignored it, hoping she would get
the hint. It didn't work that way." Mike paused and
Becca waited patiently. "She made a move on me and
kissed me. That's when her mom walked in and started
screaming. I didn't know what to do. I was afraid of
destroying my career before it even started. So, when
her mom screamed 'statutory rape,' I just gave in and

did whatever she said. She insisted on an engagement. I convinced her that I wouldn't get married until after I was finished with college. For some reason, she agreed to that. She thought the wedding should be when I graduated from UCLA. I convinced her that I couldn't get a decent job without a Master's, which is true. So, we agreed that after I finished my MS, I'd move back to California and marry her daughter. Then she wouldn't press charges. I thought I could learn to love her . . . until I met you. Anyway, I just went back to clear things up. And I'm really nervous."

"What did you do to clear things up?" Rebecca asked.

"I finally hired a lawyer."

"Where were your parents during all of this?"

Mike squinted and looked at the wall behind Rebecca. "Paris, I think." He shrugged and reached for another potato chip. "They were never really around much once I turned 18. In fact, they weren't around much while I was growing up. I had nannies and tutors. They didn't worry too much about me."

Rebecca couldn't imagine growing up in such an environment. Her parents had always been involved in Rebecca's life—so much so that it annoyed her. She said as much to Mike and took a chip out of the bag.

They sat for hours talking and munching on potato chips. They hadn't noticed the darkening sky.

"It's getting late," Rebecca said.

"I should get you home."

Rebecca smiled, pleased that Mike was finally opening up.

They left the valley and began the journey to Rebecca's house. Rebecca was quiet as she sat next to Mike. Without looking at him, she began to speak. "There is something I would like to tell you, but I'm afraid it'll have to wait," she said.

"Why?" Mike asked.

"Because I have to wait for the right moment."

"O.K." Mike signed, smiling.

That night, Rebecca made dinner . . . nothing fancy just fajitas with refried beans and chips. Mike stayed to eat while Stefan went back to his mom's place. After they washed the dishes, Mike said his goodbyes. Rebecca escorted him to the door. "Will you go out on a date with me, Becca?" he asked formally in sign language.

"Yes, I will, Mike," Becca answered just as formally.

"I'll come pick you up tomorrow around 8."

"Can you make it the day after? I've got something going on tomorrow evening," Rebecca answered. She had band rehearsal but wasn't yet ready to reveal to Mike that she sang with a band.

Mike looked surprised but then smiled. "All right. Two days, then. I'll text you tomorrow instead." He took Rebecca by the elbow and pulled her close. She circled her arms around his waist. He bent down and kissed her. *Our second kiss*, Becca thought. It seemed like things were clicking into place.

Mike and Becca continued dating, but as she kept the secret about the band, he became worried that she was still seeing Stefan. She kept her job at the restaurant and worked every day.

The day of the Talent Show arrived. Mike wanted to go bowling, but she had to tell him no.

"Why not?" he asked, getting angry.

"Well, because I have plans." She reveled in making him worry.

"But it's the Fourth of July, and I want to be with my girl! I thought we'd go bowling and then hang out at the park afterward and wait for the fireworks to start.

"Well, we can still do that, but I'm not going bowling with you. I have something to do before we can go to the park."

Mike rolled his eyes and then nodded. "Fine," he said. "We'll do it your way."

"Okay. So, meet me at the park around 3:00. We'll hang out and have some fun before the fireworks start at 9:00. Okay?"

"What am I supposed to do the rest of the day?" he asked, looking like a little lost boy.

"I don't know. Go work at the restaurant with Stefan or something," she joked.

Mike glared at her. Mike and Stefan weren't fighting anymore, but they didn't really hang out with each other either. Mike would meet Rebecca after her shift. She worked most mornings and left several evenings free for rehearsing with the band.

Mike's time was spent tutoring part-time (mostly boys this time), fixing up his house, and taking a summer class to help finish his degree in the next school year. They would both be attending NAU: Rebecca for her Bachelor's and Mike for his Master's. They were excited to be going to school at the same place and at the same time.

♪♪♪

The day of the talent show was on the Fourth of July, and it was a huge event in Flagstaff. Thousands of people gathered at the city park, hung out by the pond, picnicked on the grounds, and camped in the campgrounds. The park sported an amphitheater where the bands would compete for the right to record their music at Coconino Recording Studio and have their original music played on the radio.

There were three rounds. The first two rounds consisted of seven bands playing a cover song of their choice. Genres varied between rock and roll, modern pop, reggae, and country music. Bands were given a score, and by the end of the rounds, the bands with the highest scores moved to the third round, where they would play an original piece. If needed for a tiebreaker, the remaining bands would play an encore of another original piece. Although some bands were featured, like Becca's band, there was still a chance anyone could take home the prize. Not only were bands battling, but some featured professional bands played between sets. And of course, with music, there was food and drinks. Booths of every kind of food dotted the landscape: turkey legs, cotton candy, elephant ears, Navajo tacos, and so much more. The local breweries were even out with their beers.

That morning, Rebecca helped at the café, and then around 10:00, she met the band at the college to rehearse their pieces. Rebecca was nervous, and the ringing in her ears seemed louder than ever. She struggled to stay on key, but she hoped that the adrenaline would help by the time she was on stage. She made sure that all of the band members tuned to the correct frequency.

"The audience will be applauding and screaming," Christy reminded her. They're not subdued like they were at the café. That might interfere with the vibrations you'll feel from the band. And it might interfere with the app."

"I've got my watch set to keep time with the band. If they keep the beat consistent, then it'll be fine. We have to play it exactly like we rehearsed," Rebecca told the band. She hoped and prayed it would be okay. "I've also got the microphone set to go directly into my tablet, so the app registers what's coming from the mic and not the audience."

"Okay. Let's just hope the technology doesn't fail us like it did that one time at the café."

They had played a few times at the café, and it hadn't gone perfectly. The timing had gotten off, but Rebecca had stayed on key. She had kept her eyes on the tuner. She had also found a karaoke app that showed the words in the proper rhythm and showed her if she was in key. This worked perfectly on mute. The band would play the piece, and she would watch the words and the tuner on her tablet.

At first, Mr. Walker thought she needed the tablet for the words, but when they explained what they were doing, he provided a teleprompter for the band. As a long-time friend of Mr. Kendall, he wanted to see Rebecca succeed. The teleprompter would show the app functions from Becca's tablet, but it didn't look as conspicuous as a music stand because it was clear. People had barely noticed it was there.

Noon finally arrived, and they were scheduled for a sound check. She double-checked the grounds to make sure Mike wasn't around. He wasn't. Rebecca was glad he stuck to their timeline. He should arrive an hour before they were scheduled to play. The band had it all worked out: they would meet Rebecca casually around 3:30 and then act like they were all going for some food. Rebecca would follow saying she had to go to the bathroom, and then they would appear on stage while Mike watched. Rebecca hoped it would work.

Close to 3, Mike texted that he had arrived at the park. She met him at the gate, and they found a seat at the amphitheater. Rebecca loved the spot. The amphitheater seats were grass and sloped gently with different levels up to the edge of the stage. A concrete orchestra pit separated the grounds from the stage, which had a white band shell that extended over the stage. Two backstage doors opened up to concrete stairs that led under the bandshell. This is where the bands dressed and prepared for their music. This is where Becca's band hung out until it was time to pick up Becca from Mike's side.

Mike and Becca were sitting on a blanket enjoying the day. One of the band contestants had just finished playing a Garth Brooks' song. The crowd was receptive, but the judges didn't seem to like it. They awarded them only 60 out of 100 points. Rebecca felt bad for the band but was also hopeful that perhaps her own band would do better. So as not to cause suspicion, Becca had worn jean cut offs and a white t-shirt . . . appropriate for a day at the park, but not for playing a talent show. Her outfit, a white peasant top with pink flowers and ripped jeans with rhinestones, was in the green room under the stage.

Like clockwork, Christy and the band members walked up to Rebecca as if they were shocked to see her. "Imagine seeing you here!" Christy said.

"Hi!" Becca said. "You brought the gang!"

She introduced the band members to Mike, although he knew Richard, and they all laughed about the coincidence of running into each other at such a large event. Then they all decided to head out for some food when Becca said she had to go to the bathroom.

"I'm sorry to leave you alone," Becca said, "but do you mind staying with our stuff? I'll be back soon."

Just then, Stefan walked up.

"Oh. Hi, Stefan," Becca said. She hadn't told him about the plan and hoped he wouldn't ruin the surprise she had in mind for Mike.

"Hi, Rebecca. Could I talk to you for a minute?" he asked.

"Hmm . . . sure. I was just about to . . . walk with me," she said as she pointed towards the stage. She hoped the bathrooms were that way, too . . . just to make it realistic.

Out of earshot of Mike, Becca told Stefan about the plan and that she had to get ready.

"Ah," he said. "So, you and Mike, huh . . . you're really an item?"

Rebecca nodded. "I love him, Stefan. I'm sorry if that hurts you."

Stefan smiled a weak smile and then bent down to kiss Rebecca on the cheek. "I guess I really have lost you, then," he said.

"You never really had me, Stefan. You'll always be like my brother, and that can't change. I don't want it to. In a way, that's more special than a boyfriend. You're my family, and I hope that you'll always be there even when I'm married and have a gaggle of kids or something."

They both laughed, and Stefan hugged Rebecca. "I'm really proud of you," he said. "I know I said I would help you with your dream, but you did it all on your own."

"Well," Rebecca said, "not completely. I needed help, and you helped me along with Christy and the band. Now, I just need to show everyone that I can sing."

Stefan nodded. "You got this." He said and gave Becca a final hug before she ran down the stairs to change into her outfit.

Mike had been fidgeting with the blanket wondering where Becca was when he heard the announcer say, "And now, the next band we have on tap is Becca and the Dreamcatchers!

He couldn't believe it when he saw Becca come up on stage with the group of friends she had just introduced to him: even Richard and Christy. She had changed into ripped jeans, high heels, and a white peasant top with pink flowers. She looked beautiful.

Just then Stefan came up to him.

"Did you know about this?" Mike asked.

Stefan nodded and then sat down next to Mike on the blanket. "Let's listen," he said.

"They got the name wrong!" Christy complained, but what Christy didn't know was that Becca had changed it before they went on stage. The crowd applauded politely at first, but after the band started playing "Hotel California," the crowd was on their feet. The technology worked perfectly, and Rebecca was able to follow along with the app. She felt the vibrations of the band under her feet through the floor, and her watch buzzed in time, too. She ignored the audience and focused on the app and the vibrations in her throat.

She also kept the song in her mind, only thinking about the song and the music as she sang. She wouldn't let anything distract her.

Mike couldn't believe what he was hearing. The guitarist started the song with the famous guitar lick, and Rebecca held back until it was time for her to sing. She stepped forward with the mic in her hand, and started singing the lyrics. "On a dark desert highway . . ."

The words rang across the audience, and her pitch was spot on. Christy sang harmony . . . their voices blended perfectly. Mike loved the sultry sound of Becca's voice: she even swiveled her hips and twisted down on some of the lower notes. Mike stood applauding, amazed by what he saw and heard. He had no idea Becca was working on such a piece. It was perfect for her. Some of the lines she spoke, not needing to stay on key. What really amazed him was her stage presence. Not only could she sing, but she knew how to entertain the audience by flirting with the guitar players and dancing.

After the song ended, the crowd screamed their approval. The judges followed suit giving the band a 90 out of 100. Even with such a high score, the crowd booed it. There were several bands left, though, so Mike figured they had to leave some room for the others.

Becca came back to where Mike had been sitting. He sat her down and screamed, "You were fantastic! I can't believe it! I knew you could sing, but I had no idea you were working on such a thing! You have a band! You're a rock star!"

Becca laughed. "Not yet," she said, "but I'm working on it."

"How?" Mike asked.

"You're the one who gave me that tuning app. I just played with it, and then I found this karaoke app that showed the lyrics and whether or not I was in tune. I just kept practicing, and so did the band. We've been practicing for months."

Richard approached, and Mike punched him in the arm playfully. "And you didn't tell me you were playing in her band!? Wow!"

They milled about on the grass listening to the other bands until the first round ended. To their surprise, they made it to the second round. They chose Tracy Chapman's Song "One Reason to Stay Here." It was another excellent song for Becca's sultry, wobbly voice. She stayed on key and slid up and down the notes like an expert singer. She kept a sexy look on her face and twisted up and down the microphone stand as if she'd been a performer her entire life. She had been singing her entire life: in church, in the shower, and in the car for as long as she had a voice. From there, she had taken music lessons in guitar and voice. With that musical ability, she developed perfect pitch. She heard the sounds in her head and knew what note it was. It wasn't until she had told Mike that fateful day that she could hear the notes in her head that he realized she could sing even if she couldn't hear herself.

The third round was down to just five bands, and they would have to pick the top three bands for 1st, 2nd, and 3rd place. This was the true test of talent because the bands could no longer choose a cover song. They had to sing an original piece. Mike worried for them, not knowing what song they had written or what Becca would sing.

"Just remember," he told her, "your goal was to get here. If you win, that's just frosting."

Becca smiled. It didn't matter whether she won or lost. Everything she wanted was right here. She ran onto stage, her music pulsating in her head and her heart. And then she sang with everything she had.

The song started with a slow beat that quickly turned to a guitar solo full of fast arpeggios and then a fast fall and a screeching halt. The drum kept beat in the background—a deep bass drum that Mike could feel in the pit of his stomach. He was sure Becca felt it, too.

Then she started singing a slow, haunting tune. "I had a dream . . . But then this tragic thing . . . " The guitar started in and the lights came up and shone on Becca, who was playing a guitar. It reminded Mike of hearing her sing for the first time in that recording studio. Her voice had been sweet and quiet then, and it was sweet now, but it was full of confidence and power. She had truly found her voice.

The song continued. "I had you . . . didn't know what to do . . . .You're gone . . . And all I want's a song. I hide away . . . 'fraid a what people say . . . Maybe I'm as good as new. Maybe I should be thrown away."

The bass guitar cut in and played a solo that spun the melody high on the scale and then dropped it down to a low hum. Becca continued. "Maybe I'm as good as new . . . Maybe even better . . . 'Cuz I have another friend . . . taking care of me . . . setting me free . . . . Setting me free."

The song went back to the opening again and Mike recognized a bridge. "I won't forget you now . . . but somehow . . . I found a way to live without you . . . " Then the melody circled around back to the chorus. "I have another friend . . . taking care of me . . . setting me free . . . Setting me freeeeee." Becca held the final note that faded into nothing as the drum rolled underneath the sound until there was silence.

The audience roared, and Mike wished Becca could hear it. She saw it, he knew . . . saw her smiling, saw the tears glistening in her eyes. She knew what she had just done.

She ran off stage, and as the other bands played, she ran to Mike's side.

"I love you," he signed, and then he whispered it for her to see. He could shout it from the San Francisco Peaks and still not feel like she could understand how much he meant it.

"I love you, too," she said and kissed him as she cried. "Thank you for helping me make my dream come true."

"Marry me," he blurted, getting down on one knee. He pulled out a black box and opened it to reveal a single round diamond in a gold setting. "Marry me." He repeated. "The house is yours. It was always meant for us. For you and me and maybe our children. Marry me."

Rebecca cried just as Christy pulled her away. "It's our turn again! We're tied for first. They want an encore!!" Christy shouted.

They left Mike kneeling on the ground, his smile bright.

On stage, Becca spoke as the crowd quieted down. A stage hand brought her a stool, and she sat on it with her guitar balanced on one knee. "This wasn't planned. We had another song in mind, one written by Christy, my best friend. But if we win, you'll get to hear it on our album."

The crowd cheered, and Becca went on. "But there's a man on his knee out there waiting for an answer. This is what I have to say."

Her fingers strummed the guitar, and the audience fell silent.

Someday my love will come.
Someday he'll come through the rain.
He will smile, then say my name.
I will know who he is
I will know he is the one I've waited for.
Someday my love will come.
Someday we will shine as one.
He will take me from this world.
He will bring me peace.
I will stay by his side . . . forever.

THE END

Song 1

I had you
Didn't know what to do
You're gone
And all I want's a song.
I hide away
'Fraid a what people say
Maybe I'm as good as new.
Maybe I should be thrown away.
Maybe I'm as good as new.   Maybe even better
'Cuz I have another friend
Taking care of me.
Setting me free.
Setting me free.
I won't forget you now.
But somehow I found
A way to live without you.

Chorus

'Cuz I have another friend
Taking care of me.
Setting me free.
Setting me free.
'Cuz I have another friend
Setting me free.

Encore song
Someday my love will come.
Someday he'll come through the rain.
He will smile, then say my name.
I will know who he is
I will know he is the one I've waited for.
Someday my love will come.
Someday we will shine as one.
He will take me from this world.
He will bring me peace.
I will stay by his side . . . forever.

American Sign Language Alphabet

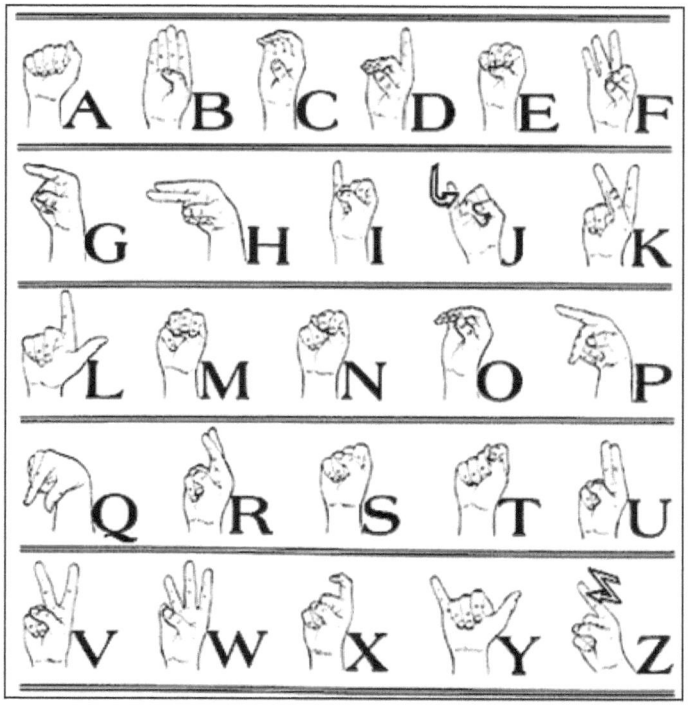

By Jazz Davis (Own work) [CC BY-SA 4.0 (http://creativecommons.org/licenses/by-sa/4.0)], via Wikimedia Commons.

Acknowledgements

Writing is a solitary activity, but getting published takes a host of people. I want to thank all those who helped me get this book out to you. First of all, I want to thank my husband, Matt, who put up with my emotional ups and downs. I also want to thank my mom who believed in me my whole life, Papa who told me I could be anything I wanted, and Dad for giving me the love of music. I also want to thank my editor, Claire Shepherd whose eagle eyes caught many of the 14-year-old errors I still make. And thank you to Yvonne Osborne who said, "Go for it!" Thank you to Diana Gabaldon who inspires me every day to be a better writer.

About the Author

Keri De Deo first wrote this story as a teenager living in Nebraska. As a musician, she wondered what it would be like to be a deaf musician. Would she still be able to sing? Having been raised to believe "where there is a will, there is a way," she wanted to find out how one would survive such a "tragedy." These thoughts inspired this story.

Keri De Deo is a writer, E-learning Consultant, ESL and Composition instructor, and an accomplished musician. She is the owner/operator of Witty Owl Consulting.

www.keridedeo.com

www.ingramcontent.com/pod-product-compliance
Lightning Source LLC
Chambersburg PA
CBHW051842170626
46807CB00003B/1305